Into the Deep End

By

Stone Cruz

Weeping Rose Books
Published by Indigo Sea Press
Winston-Salem

Weeping Rose Books
Indigo Sea Press
PO Box 67201
Winston-Salem, NC 27114

This book is a work of fiction. Names, characters, locations and events are either a product of the author's imagination, fictitious or used fictitiously. Any resemblance to any event, locale or person, living or dead, is purely coincidental.

For information regarding bulk purchases of this book, digital purchase and special discounts, please contact the publisher at indigoseapress@gmail.com

Cover design by Pan Morelli
Manufactured in the United States of America
ISBN 978-1-63066-473-2

To Laura, dearest friend and confidant.

Chapter One

"Laura, there's a man by my pool."

"Oh my god! Is he trying to get into your house?"

"No. He's doing something to the water in the pool."

Her friend paused, struggling to understand and also to wake up. "Wait. What? Didn't you call a pool company for a quote yesterday?"

"Yes."

"Did it ever occur to you that this guy might be with that pool company?"

"Oh, I know he is," Wendy said. "It says 'Bolden Pools' on the back of his shirt."

". . . You called me at 7 a.m. to tell me a somebody showed up to take care of your pool?"

"Be serious, Laura. What legitimate pool company shows up at 7 a.m.? In the winter? Anyway, you always say I can call you whenever I need to."

"There is no winter in Orlando, Wendy. Just too-cool-to-get-in-the-pool. How should I know what time of day they start? Maybe they start early and finish by noon. What's he doing?"

"He undid the end of the pool cover by the house and he's dipping things in the water."

"How unusual. Isn't that exactly what pool maintenance people do?"

"That's just it. I didn't ask them to do anything. I just wanted a quote on how much it would cost me a month for them to take care of the pool. I'm afraid they sent this guy early to do a bunch of stuff and then charge me for it without my permission."

"Oh for Christ's sake, Wendy. You woke me up for this?" Her friend was clearly peeved and tired. "Instead of bothering

1

me with this, why don't you open the freaking kitchen door and ask him what he's doing?"

"I can't do that. I'm not downstairs. I'm upstairs in my bedroom looking out the window. And, anyway, I'm just in a t-shirt and panties."

Laura chuckled. "Go shake those classic titties at him, sweetie. That pool man will do anything you ask him."

"That's just it. I don't want him to do anything."

"Well then put on your robe and go downstairs and talk to the man."

". . . I'm going to call the pool company. If they send out people at 7 a.m., chances are somebody's already in the office. I'll ask them what this guy is doing. And if nobody's there, I'll leave a message and tell them I'm not paying for anything I didn't authorize."

"You do that, girl." Her friend was clearly tired of talking. "I'm going back to bed."

Her back to the window. Wendy scrolled through the call log of her cellphone until she came to a number she didn't recognize and assumed it was the pool company. She hit the redial button. As it rang, she went to the window and looked down at the man below, who appeared to be making notations on a clipboard.

"Bolden Pools. This is Garrett."

"Uh, yes, this is Mrs.—" She caught herself. As of the last two days she wasn't Toffler anymore. She was Marbury again. "This is Ms. Marbury. Wendy Marbury."

"How are you this morning, Ms. Marbury?"

"I'm—I'm—I'm just fine, thank you. Uh, I think one of your pool men is in my backyard."

"One of our men?"

"Yes."

"What does he look like?"

"Um. He's wearing a blue shirt that says 'Bolden Pools' on the back and khaki shorts and topsiders."

2

"I think I know who you're talking about, ma'am. Is he in his mid-30s? Does he have a kind of scruffy, half-grown beard? Looks like he could use a shave?"

"Well, I can't see his face really."

"Oh that's all right. Frankly he's not much to look at. Is he disturbing you?"

"Oh no," Wendy said. "He's over by the pool. He's doing something in the water."

"He's doing something in the water?"

"Nothing bad, I mean."

"Ms. Marbury, are you at 1008 Ocala Lane?"

"Yes. That's my address."

"Well I have a note here that yesterday you left a voice mail requesting a quote for regular pool service."

The man by the pool with his back to the house held up what looked like a test tube, gazing at it in the early sun.

"I wanted a quote, yes," she said. "I'm not ready to sign a contract yet or have any work done on the pool."

"Oh, I see. . . . Let me assure you that fellow isn't there to treat the pool or do any work on it, ma'am. He's simply running some tests on the water to see what condition it's in."

"Oh?"

"Yes. From the chemical makeup of the water and a visual inspection of the sides of the pool itself, he'll be able to tell if any significant work needs to be done to keep the pool crystal clear and safe."

Wendy had a little sinking feeling. As she listened to the explanation of all they did before giving a quote, she decided this pool company sounded expensive.

She sighed. "Well . . . nobody has done anything, really, with the pool since the first of October. So that's . . . six months. My husband—my ex-husband—took care of it until we quit using it for the season and since then it's just . . ."

"Fallow? The pool has been left to fend for itself?"

"Yes. . . . I don't know how much I can afford to do any

extra upkeep and maintenance."

The man below pulled the pool cover back into place and fastened it. He stood and continued making notes.

"Perhaps it won't take a lot of work, Ms. Marbury. Our man can assess any needed cleaning, determine if the water needs to be shocked and set up a chemical regimen to make it fairly simple and inexpensive to keep the pool in good shape until you're ready to swim."

"He can do all that economically?" she asked skeptically?

"Oh yes, ma'am. He's quite capable. In fact he can do all that while he's talking on the phone."

The fellow by the pool turned toward the house and looked directly at the upstairs window, where Wendy stood before the glass in nothing but her pink t-shirt and aqua panties.

She gasped. Phone still pressed to her ear, she tried to lower the shade, fumbling helplessly with the twine. She looked back down to find him staring up at her, his phone protruding from his ear, and she jumped to the side, her back to the bedroom wall where she could not be seen.

"... Ms. Marbury? . . . Are you still on the line?"

". . . Yes."

"I'm sorry if I startled you ma'am. My name is Garrett Bolden. I'm the owner of the pool service and I do all estimates for the company. I do try to give the best service possible at the best price we can manage. Now, uh, it will only take me a few minutes to finish this quote and, if it's not too great an imposition, I could show it to you. . . . You have some alternatives as to the cost if you're trying to keep your expenses to a minimum."

She leaned slowly toward the window and glimpsed the pool man writing on his clipboard. "So you're saying you want to talk to me and give me a quote right now?"

"If that's convenient for you, yes ma'am. If not I can make arrangements to come back later after I finish my other appointments. I would like to discuss the condition of the pool personally and go over our estimate and your options. Whether you go with Garrett Pools or someone else, I think it's important for you to know exactly what shape the water's in."

"Well, uh . . . can you give me, like, two minutes?"

"Yes ma'am."

"I'll unlock that door right there by you. That's the kitchen."

"Yes ma'am."

She dropped her cell onto the bed and scurried across the room to her closet.

"Oh man," she muttered. "Who ever heard of doing business at 7 a.m.?" She pushed aside the hangered dresses, slacks and blouses looking for the robe she never wore. "If this were a different time zone, then 7 a.m. would make sense." She found it, pink and looking a little tattered, near the end of the rack. "It least in this my nipples won't show. Does he really have that many quotes to give? In March?"

She pulled on the robe, stepped into her slippers and headed down the stairs.

"Seriously. I'm not going to be able to afford this. I know it." She turned from the bottom landing toward the kitchen. "I just want to know if the water has turned to pure algae. How green is it?"

Tightening her robe about her and tying the belt, she unlocked the deadbolt on the kitchen door and pulled it open. Standing just outside, clipboard in hand, was the man from Bolden Pools. He looked up at her as she caught sight of him.

He was not, she decided instantly, "not much to look at," as he had described himself. In fact he was a lot to look at: well-muscled, average height, slender and tan with a shock of dark brown hair and the beginnings of a beard he obviously kept closely trimmed. Instantly she put a hand atop her head, pushing back her blonde locks and wondering how she looked with no makeup and uncombed hair.

"Ms. Marbury?"

5

"Mr. Bolden?"

"Yes, ma'am. Just call me Garrett, please. May I come in?"

Wendy moved aside and he stepped into the kitchen. One hand holding the top of her robe closed, she motioned toward the kitchen table.

"Thank you," he said quietly.

He pulled out a chair and set the clipboard on the table. She sat down opposite him, watching as he added a column of figures.

She heard steps on coming down the stairs and started to warn whichever of her daughters was descending that a strange man was in the house. Only she wasn't sure how to say it.

Sleepy and frumpy, barefoot, her short blonde hair sticking out in a dozen directions, and wearing a beige pajama top and pink panties, thirteen-year-old Tina came into the kitchen in full whine mode. "Mom, you were supposed to wake me—"

She gasped and jumped when she saw Garrett, and when she did her small breasts jiggled in unison beneath her top. Instantly she put both arms across her chest. She turned and ran toward the stairs, reaching one hand behind her to shield her bottom. Tina gave a little shriek as she dashed up the stairs.

For a few seconds neither of the adults sitting at the kitchen table spoke. They looked at each other.

"Well, Mr. Bolden. . . Garrett. In less than five minutes you've seen two thirds of the females in this house in their underwear."

He gazed at her for a moment, reflecting. "Ms. Marbury, I apologize for any embarrassment I've caused. I truly do not mean to be intrusive or insensitive, or to take advantage." He drew a breath. "In my line of work, I see people in bathing suits constantly. I would note that underwear usually covers more of the body than a bathing suit does and yet, while we

6

are not ashamed to be seen in a bathing suit, we are always embarrassed to be seen in our underwear." He nodded. "Of course that will not change the fact that your daughter feels scandalized and maybe violated right now."

Wendy shrugged. "Tina's thirteen. She has the 'worst possible thing in the world' happen to her about three times a day. It can't be helped."

"I do apologize. Now about your pool."

"Yes."

"It seems to me that you are quite concerned about containing cost when it comes to upkeep of the pool, correct?"

She sighed. "Yes, Mr.—Garrett. I have just gone through a divorce. Being a mother with two minor children, I ended up with the house—which is good. But I also ended up with the expenses of the house. Now I'm not destitute. In fact I'm an accountant and I mostly work from home. Also, as you might imagine, I'm really good with budgets. And that means I know how much I can afford to spend on keeping up the pool. I also know that I don't know a whole lot about keeping the pool swimmable—if that's a word." He smiled and she smiled and continued. "Aaron was always out there piddling with it. At least it seemed like it. And the result was, well, beautiful. The water was always clear. The problem is, I never learned anything about taking care of it. And I've seen pools that haven't been cared for. The water gets disgusting. It stinks. The pool itself can get discolored."

"Well," Garrett said, "it's unhealthy. People can get really sick swimming in unclean water."

She drew a breath. "So I'm sort of between a rock and hard place. I know I need to keep the pool clean and need some professional help to do it, but I don't have a lot budgeted for that."

Garrett leaned back in his chair, considering her words. She expected him to ask what amount she had budgeted to take care of the swimming pool, but he didn't.

"Actually I have a pretty good idea of what you're going through, Ms. Marbury."

"Wendy. If I call you Garrett, you call me . . ."

"Wendy. Yes ma'am. I understand what it is to have to divide things when couples go their separate ways and sometimes the amount of income one spouse has doesn't match up with the responsibilities that spouse is faced with."

"Oh. Cool. Thank you for knowing that."

He nodded. "So first let me say that, for having been unattended for several months, the pool is not in real bad condition."

"It's not?"

"Not terrible, no. It's like your husband seemed to have an idea he wasn't going to be cleaning it and he did a good job of shutting it down for the season. And, also, it was fallow over the winter—to the extent that we have winter in Florida— which is a lot better than leaving one without treatment all summer."

A wave of relief spread through her. "Well that's good news."

"It is. Yes. That said, your pool is pretty good sized and does need to be shocked and then well-chlorinated for . . ." He gazed at her. "When do you usually start swimming in it? First of May?"

"Yes. I think about then. Typically maybe the middle of May. My girls love the pool and all their friends love our pool, but they get cold easily. They're just skinny little things."

Garrett made a note on his clipboard. "Well," he said, "without looking up. That gives us sixty days to make it perfect." He looked back up at Wendy. "So here is what we can do to make it as affordable as possible. First, let's figure out the process. Let's say that we need some special chemicals to shock the pool right away. They're not too expensive. About $25. Then let's say we are going to one time do a cleaning to make the tile and the bottom shine. After that, we'll show you how to set up the automatic sweep and to check the chlorine level every day. Then one of our guys will come over once every two weeks to check everything and do any necessary cleaning."

Visions of dollar signs began to roll before her eyes. Without having heard a number, Wendy was already certain her budget was blown. And if she couldn't afford to keep the pool clean, she might actually have to work with Aaron to sell the house.

"Also," he continued, "we'll give you a list of chemicals and test supplies you'll need. When we get through here, if it's okay, I'll check inside your pool storage building to see what you have and what you'll need. Now, with these chemicals, instead of buying them from me, just get them at a building supply or a superstore. I have to mark it up and it's cheaper for you if you buy them there."

"Okay."

"So now let's talk about finances and timing."

". . . Okay."

He studied her face. He had the slight glimmer of a smile, and maybe something else behind it as well.

"Let's say we send you a bill at the end of this month for the chemicals and the cleaning. And let's say we come over once more before the end of the month to check on things and make sure the pool is on track to be ready for this summer. So the bill will be for $25 for the chemicals and $50 for the two visits by our pool men. That would be a total of $75 for March."

She felt her jaw drop. ". . . A total of $75?"

He nodded slowly, "Which will be due and payable at the end of April. For April and beyond, for the two visits by our pool guys, we'll bill you $50 a month. Would that work?"

Slowly she said, "Are you kidding me, Mr. Bolden? That's it?"

"I've been in your position, Ms. Marbury."

A gradual, irresistible smile altered her expression, and with it came a tremendous sense of relief and gratitude.

"You are very kind. . . . And please, Garrett, do call me Wendy."

They heard another set of footsteps descending the stairs. Wendy could not imagine that Tina—even fully dressed—could bring herself to appear before this stranger again. And she was right. Appearing through the kitchen door, wearing what she called her "Scotch outfit"—red blouse and checkered skirt with black leggings—ten-year-old Tasha stood with her arms folded across her chest and a look of grave suspicion on her face.

"My sister said there was a man in the kitchen."

Garrett's eyebrows arched. "And here I am."

"Who are you?"

"My name is Garrett. I clean swimming pools."

"Are you going to clean our pool?"

"Yes he is," Wendy said. "And you are to call him Mr. Bolden."

Tasha considered the man sitting before her, squinting as she decided what she was going to say next.

"My mom is divorced now, you know."

Wendy felt her jaw drop.

"I see," Garrett said. "And how do you feel about that?"

"Oh!" Tasha rolled her eyes, dropping her hands to her hips. "I'm just so glad it's over. That's all I've heard about for months."

"Well," Garrett replied with a shrug, "important things take a lot of time."

"Are you divorced?" the girl asked accusingly.

"Tasha!"

"I am, as a matter of fact."

She squinted at him again. "You got any kids?"

"Not a one."

"Why not?"

"Tasha!"

"Because the lady I was married to wouldn't let me name one 'Tasha.'"

The girl was silent, deciding whether or not she was being teased. "Well it's actually 'Nuh-tau-sha.'"

"Natasha," Garrett said. "Maybe she would have let me name one 'Natasha.' What grade are you in?"

"Fourth. I'm ten. Just had a birthday."

"Excellent. And what grade is your sister in?"

"Seventh. She's thirteen."

Garrett nodded. "Are you ready for school?"

Tasha shook her head. "I haven't had breakfast."

"Tasha," Wendy broke in, "go upstairs and tell your sister we are leaving in fifteen—make it ten—minutes for school. We're going to stop at the arches for breakfast this morning."

"Sweet!" she exclaimed and dashed from the room.

The adults watched her disappear and then faced one another again across the table.

"I'm afraid I've been a major disruption in your morning routine, ma'am."

"Actually," she said slowly, "you may not realize it, the girls certainly don't know it, but you have pretty much saved the house for us. If I couldn't have figured out inexpensive pool care, I was going to have to sell the property, split the proceeds with my ex and find a cheaper place to live."

Garrett nodded. "Yes ma'am. I'm familiar with that drill." He stood. "Would it be possible for me to drop back by sometime this evening or this afternoon to do an initial treatment of the pool. I'll have a list of things you need to make sure you have going forward and I'll go over the daily testing of the pool."

"That would be great."

"Okay." He nodded. "I'll bring a contract. You don't have to sign it right away. Take your time and read it and make sure it covers everything you want and that the price works for you."

"I'm sure it will be fine. I'm very appreciative."

"What's the best time for me to drop by?"

An odd thrill twirled in her chest. "Um. Well. How about, say, 1:30? Is that too early?"

"Not at all. I'll see you then. I'll let myself out the door here if you want to lock it behind me. I look forward to seeing you this afternoon."

Chapter Two

The instant Wendy heard Garrett's tap on the kitchen door, she felt the same little electric surge in her chest she had experienced that morning when they set up their appointment. As she hopped up from the table and went to the door, she asked herself when she had last felt that thrill.

She remembered the first time. It was her first kiss. In the spring of her eighth grade year, she and her boyfriend, Randy Meeker, hid together beneath the aluminum bleachers in the middle school gymnasium. They had stared at each other for ten or fifteen seconds, then kissed. Wendy had been instantly sure that theirs was a timeless love. A couple days later they had done it again, but the amazing thrill hadn't happened.

When had she felt that fluttering excitement with her ex-husband Aaron? She couldn't remember that she ever had.

Garrett Bolden stood before her, satchel of pool supplies in one hand and a packet of information in the other. His mouth dropped open for an instant when he saw her and Wendy knew she had overdressed.

Because he had so obviously reacted to her, apparently Garrett thought he needed to say something. "That's a very nice outfit," he said in a sedate tone. "You look . . . very attractive."

She felt herself blush—another rare occurrence for her—and smiled at him. "Well, even though I work in my house, I didn't want you to get the idea that I sit around all day in a tattered, old bathrobe."

He gazed again at her tight coral top and the white Capri slacks that revealed her shape so well. "You look very nice," he nodded. "We need to make sure we don't get chlorine on your clothes. It will eat right through them."

They stared at each other. Then she spoke up. "Where do you want to start?"

"Uh. Let me show you how to check the water in the pool and turn on the skimmer."

"Skimmer?"

She followed him onto the cement apron of the pool and watched him drop to one knee and test the chemistry of the water, trying to listen as he explained—in what she realized were fairly simple, comprehensible terms—what he was doing and what he wanted her to do every day. It was difficult for her to concentrate, she decided, because she was so focused on Garrett.

What was she thinking? Well, she knew what she was thinking—but why was she thinking it? Was this some kind of a new freedom she was diving into now that she was divorced? Was this the famous "rebound" that happened to so many people when a long-term relationship ended? All she knew for sure was that she was having a hard time paying attention to the instructions he was trying to give her.

"You wrote this all down, right?"

"Yes, ma'am," he said, handing her the thick manila envelope. "Everything is in there: instructions, contact information and the contract."

He led her to the pool house where the pump, pool toys and chemicals were kept.

"So this was all very well organized," he said, standing in the doorway. "It's like your husband—I'm sorry, ex-husband—was setting things up so someone like me wouldn't have any trouble finding what he needed and locating the supplies you already have." He turned to her. "Is he an accountant too?"

"No." She shook her head. "He is an engineer."

"Ah," Garrett responded, nodding. "That explains the compulsive organizing."

"I guess."

"I saw this morning that you actually had most of the supplies you're going to need to keep the pool in good shape until June or even July."

"That is good," Wendy said. "You have no idea how stressed out I was. I was afraid the pool was going to be a swamp and it was going to cost me hundreds of dollars to get it ready for the summer."

He didn't look at her. He seemed to be deciding what he wanted to ask her.

"Well, if your ex wasn't going to at least help you get the pool treated, I take it this wasn't the friendliest divorce?"

"Well," she replied, "it wasn't totally acrimonious. . . . I guess you'd say it more a case of neglect than abuse. He pretty much just demonstrated that he could care less about me. At the same time he didn't want to alienate the girls."

"Did he want to fight over custody—if you don't mind my asking?"

"No and no. Tina and Tasha are an inconvenience for him most of the time. He has them every other weekend, so he can lavish paternal wisdom and affection on them."

"I see. And the girls really love and miss their dad?"

"Mostly they feel disdain. They knew, long before he left us, that he was full of shit."

Garrett laughed. "And—this isn't any of my business— did he leave you for someone else?" He closed the pool house door.

"No, actually. Not that he hasn't had girlfriends." She turned with him and started back toward the house. "I guess I'd say, he didn't leave me for someone else. He left me for anyone else."

He laughed again, shaking his head. "I know you were making a joke. I hope it's okay that I laughed at it."

"Why not? I do. Aren't you going to electrocute my pool?"

"Shock it? No, ma'am. I got here about fifteen minutes before I knocked on the door. I've already treated the pool."

"Oh. . . . Oh." A wave of disappointment spread through her. "That was quick. . . . Well, I was having a cup of coffee there at the kitchen table. Could I pour you a cup?"

"Caffeinated or de-caffeinated?"

"Oh. It's regular. It's got caffeine in it."

"Thank god. Sure. I'd love a cup."

There it was again, that crazy little thrill.

Wendy led him into the kitchen and pulled a mug from the cupboard as he sat in the chair beside hers.

"So, um," she began, "you sort of have the better of me. A couple times you've made reference to being divorced yourself. Are you still? Single, I mean?"

He chuckled. "Oh yes. Unlike your situation, my wife had somebody else in mind. She ended up in the divorce settlement getting the 2600 square foot house I built overlooking Lake Hart, where she lives with her girlfriend."

"Oh! . . . Oh. . . . I don't know what to say."

"Neither did I."

"So, you lost your house?"

"Well, my ex-wife co-habitates with a girl who has never wanted for money. So taking over the mortgage was not a problem for them." As she set the mug before him, he said, "Thanks. Just a little sugar is fine." He stirred the coffee, reflecting. "I ended up in a townhouse I'm renting not far from the airport. And—" There was a hint of victory in his voice. "—I managed to hang onto my boats."

"Boats? You have motorboats?"

"Oh, I have one of those. But what I really enjoy are my two sailboats."

She eased into the chair beside him. "You like to sail?"

"Yes. Very much."

"Well, uh, where do you sail?"

"On the zillion lakes around here. Sometimes I go over to the coast—the Atlantic side, usually—and sail on the big pond."

"So how often do you sail?"

"Three, maybe four times a week." He watched her,

studying the nuances of her face and expression. "That's why I get up so early. The best wind on the lakes is in the afternoon."

She stared at her mug. "Well, I guess, now it's my turn to ask you a personal question." She glanced at him from the corner of her eye. "When your ex left you, were you devastated?"

He leaned back in his chair slowly. "No. I can't say I was. I guess I was illuminated. Sherry and I had been together since we were in high school. We dated all the way through UCF and got married right after we graduated. We had been the 'cute couple' going way back. All our friends just expected us to be together and, I guess, we just followed through with what everyone was assuming." He gazed past her, reflecting. "I would say we were good partners. We both built good careers. We helped each other out. But there wasn't any real magic between us. Ever."

Her eyes widened as she thought about the electric thrills Garrett repeatedly stirred in her. Hadn't his ex-wife felt those as well?

Wendy opened the packet of documents and fished out two copies of the contract. It only took a few seconds for her to verify that all the agreements they had discussed that morning were spelled out precisely on the paper.

"This looks proper," she said absently.

"You can keep it and look it over before you sign it, if you'd like."

"Nope," she said. "I don't want to give you the chance to change your mind."

He laughed. "If it works for you, ma'am, it works for Bolden Pools."

Giving him a momentary glance—wishing he had called her "Wendy"—she got up and took a pen from the junk drawer by the refrigerator. Signing the contracts, she set aside her copy and gave the other to Garrett.

"Thanks. And thanks for the coffee."

"My pleasure," she said quietly. She didn't want him to leave, and had no good reason to delay him. "So you'll come by the weekend after next to check the water, clean and treat it?"

"Well usually I send one of the young guys over to do that. Weekend work gives me a chance to offer some hours to my part time helpers."

"Oh. Okay."

"I'll probably send Stan or Mads."

"Mads? Mads Madison?"

He looked at her. "Yeah."

"You know Marshall Madison?"

"Well yeah. I've known him since he was maybe eight or nine-years-old. I take it you know him too?"

"We only know of him by following all his swimming victories last year. So Marshall Madison works for you?"

"Yes."

"And you know him personally?"

He nodded slowly. "I pretty much know all my employees personally."

"So, if I can ask, how did you meet Mads?"

Garrett leaned back in his chair. "I was a competitive swimmer around here back in the day. And I guess some folks remembered that. So after I was out of college, one of the local clubs hit me up to coach their youngest swim team. I'd coached for six or seven years before Mads came along. The first time I saw him in the water, though, I knew a real fish when I saw one. He was not just good, but very coachable. So all this time he and I have remained close. And I let him work around his training schedule."

"Oh my god," she said slowly. "Do you still go to his swim meets?"

"Most of them."

She tilted her head. "I wonder why we haven't seen you there."

He stared at her, reflecting on her question even as the absurdity of it—why hadn't she seen someone she had never met—began to dawn on her.

"Well, often," he said, "I wear my cloak of invisibility."

She began to laugh, closing her eyes and to her own surprise, touching his hand. "That did make me sound stupid." She sighed. "I should have said, I guess I thought I would have recognized you if I had seen you at one of his swim meets. I have to tell you, my daughter adores Mads Madison."

He nodded. "Would that be the plaid skirt or the pink panties?"

She laughed again. "Tina. Miss Pink Panties. She is huge into competitive swimming and has been for four or five years now. Last year her coach told her to start going to the big high school meets to see what she could learn by watching."

"Ah. Smart coach."

"Miss Rashim. She is good. And the first one we went to last year, Tina watched Mads just destroy the competition in about five races. Before the guy dried off, she was in love."

Garrett smiled. "Mads is a terrific kid. He's a great role model and a hard worker. I'm going to be sorry to lose him."

"Lose him?" There was alarm in her voice.

"Well, he's a senior. He's got a full scholarship to Tallahassee starting this fall. I think he reports there the third week of August."

"Oh. But he'll be working for you until then?"

"Hope so."

"And . . . you think Tina might get to meet him when he comes around to service the pool."

"We can make sure of that. We'll make him your regular service man."

"Oh my god. . . . I think I could actually get Tina to pay for our pool service."

He laughed.

"So he'll come over every couple weeks on the weekend,

starting a week from Saturday?"

"Yes. He'll be your tech. Unless some sort of problem develops, you know, that requires me to come check it out."

Suddenly it dawned on her that, while Tina might want to see Mads, Wendy wanted to see Garrett.

"What kind of problem?"

"Well, the pump or the skimmer can get out of whack in ways Mads might not be able to fix. Sometime there are just electrical or plumbing issues that I have to fix."

". . . You know about plumbing?"

"Sure. Kind of comes with the territory."

"You know a lot about plumbing?"

"Yes. . . . Why do you ask?"

Her tone became sheepish. "Well, I hate to mention this, but I have a minor plumbing thing."

"Oh?"

"I should know how to fix it, but I don't. Aaron used to take care of these things and I didn't have to worry about them. I hate to call a plumber because I know it's probably minor."

His head tilted slowly to one side. "What sort of problem is it?"

"Well, upstairs we have two bathrooms. The girls' toilet wants to run intermittently. It doesn't run constantly. It just seems to fill up the tank after it's flushed and then, every few minutes, I can hear it run a little more. I don't know how the water in the tank is leaking. Late at night I can hear it run. It keeps me awake and drives me crazy. The girls could sleep through a hurricane. They don't even notice. But that little repetitive running water sound is so annoying to me."

"Well," he said, "would you like me to see if I can fix it?"

"Would you? You can add it to my monthly bill."

He chuckled as he stood up. "Why don't you show me where it is?"

They were quite close together when she stood up. She could smell the faint suntan lotion he must've rubbed on his face and the back of his neck. The feeling of his nearness made her hold her breath. As she led him up the stairs she wondered how she appeared to him from behind. Did he find her attractive? Somewhat attractive? She could not be, she knew, as attractive to him as he was to her.

She glanced involuntarily into Tasha's room as they passed it. At least the younger girl had made her bed. There were a minimum of clothes, books and toys spread about. Between the girls' room was the smaller bathroom. As if on cue, she heard the water in the toilet run and shut off as she opened the door. Misplaced toothpaste, shampoo, towels and small piles of dirty clothes made her cringe as the two grownups entered.

"Uh. Sorry for the mess. I guess the girls were in a hurry this morning."

Garrett smiled. "Your girls didn't have a warning I was coming. And they don't need to know I came up here and saw anything either."

"You're too kind, as if they'd ever notice."

He pulled the lid off the toilet and stared down into the open back of the tank. Wordlessly he flushed the handle and, as the water dropped, he unhooked the little chain that connected the arm of the float and moved it down to different tiny hole in the arm. They stood watching silently for several minutes after the tank refilled.

Finally she looked up at him. "That was it?"

He shrugged. "You said it was minor."

"I didn't know it was *that* minor."

Garrett gently placed the ceramic lid back onto the toilet. "That's why there are multiple slots in the float arm, so the ball can be adjusted up or down to get the right level of water for a flush. The way it was set, water filled the tank above the overflow tube and it kept flowing out until the ball sank enough to open the valve again."

He turned to the lavatory, squirted liquid soap on his palms and began to wash his hands. She watched him silently, wanting to think of a reason to keep him from leaving, to engage him in dialogue or activity so that he would stay longer. These were, she realized, the feelings of a schoolgirl. Still, they were undeniable.

"Why did it just start leaking like that? It worked perfectly for years."

He shrugged. "Any mechanical thing like that, especially made out of plastic, is eventually going to wear and get out of adjustment. There was nothing really wrong with it. Uh. . . . what towel do you want me to use?"

"Oh, here," she said, turning to the towel pantry. "Let me get you a clean one."

She turned to give the hand towel to him and dropped it. He tried to catch it in the air, but it fell straight to the bathroom floor. Both of them went to their knees to pick it up and Wendy grabbed it. As she held it out to him, their faces were only a few, scant inches apart. They stared at each other.

It was so like that moment under the bleachers with Randy Meeker, only this time the yearning she felt was for more than a quick, chaste kiss. She leaned forward and kissed him. It was a lingering, hopeful kiss, and when she broke away she did not pull back from him. When she opened her eyes, his were open as well, watching her. He leaned toward her slowly, putting one wet hand behind her head and pulling her lips to his, and they kissed again, a long, hot kiss that was at once satisfying for her and not nearly enough.

He took the towel from her and sat down, his back against the bathtub, drying his hands. He studied her face with longing and uncertainty.

"Really," he said, "I wasn't going to charge you for fixing your toilet."

Wendy giggled. She crawled the few inches to him and kissed him again, putting both her hands behind his head and—the passion within her overcoming her reluctance—

forcing her tongue into his mouth. They kissed for long seconds, broke to breathe, then kissed again. And as they kissed she began to unbutton his shirt and when it fell open she ran her hands inside it, felt the firmness of his chest, then looped her arms around him. Garrett put his arms around her back, pressing the two of them tightly together.

She pulled back from him and sat down. She held his shirt open, looking at his body.

"This isn't my bathroom. My bathroom is in my bedroom. . . . Want me to show you?"

He gave her a slow beautiful smile. "Actually, I've been wanting to see—hoping to see. To see everything you have. Ever since that little glimpse I got of you in your blue underwear, with your girls trying to burst right out of that t-shirt."

She gasped. "You saw that?"

Nodding slowly, he answered. "You are an amazingly arousing woman, Ms. Marbury."

Her eyes widened. "Are you amazingly aroused?"

"Oh, you have to determine that for yourself. Only, I do have one question at this instant."

"What?"

"What time do your girls get home from school."

"What time is it now?"

He glanced at his watch. "Almost 2."

"Tasha gets home first, in an hour-and-a-half. Is that enough time for everything you to see everything you want to?"

"Well it's enough time for a good start. Some things I may want to see more than once. Where did you say your bedroom was?"

She took his hand and stood. "Let me show you."

Wendy pulled him to his feet. She felt as if she were dragging him as she guided him out of the bathroom into the hall. And there he stopped her. She turned to him, full of uncertainty. Had he changed his mind? Had she been too forward?

Garrett pulled her to him, kissing her, putting his hand in the small of her back and pressing their bodies together. As she pressed her hips against him, their stomachs flat against each other, the rigidity of his penis was unmistakable. He wanted her, she realized, as she wanted him.

She pushed his shirt off his shoulders, letting it drop to the floor. In the next instant she felt his hand on her back slip beneath her top and lift it upward. They broke their kiss long enough for her to lift her arms as he pulled the blouse over her head and let it fall, then their lips and chests came back together. She felt his hand fall upon the clasp of her strapless bra in the back and undo it with an effortless motion and then pull it off her and let it fall away as well. The delicious sensation of her bare breasts against his naked chest ran through her and, surprisingly, sent a tingle through her crotch. She was, realized, quite wet already.

He did not stop kissing her as his hand moved gently to her breast. With a single, smooth fingertip he caressed a wildly enflamed nipple and she felt her shoulders droop. Her head fell backward and his lips descended to her breast, his mouth covering as much as it as he could and his tongue, rougher than his fingers, exploring the raised bumps on the areola and the erect nipple.

Her hand went to the front of his shorts, tracing the outline of his rock hard member. She squeezed it, then looped both hands around the small of his back.

"You know," she said, taking a breath, "I think you have a pretty big plumbing issue there yourself I can help you with."

He studied her face, his expression full of playful joy and arousal. "It might get pretty wet."

She swallowed. "Oh, it's already wet, Mr. Bolden."

With the smoothest, most powerful motion, he stooped and picked her up. "Sounds like something I need to check out."

She felt the power in his arms as he carried her down the hallway. Her head drooped against his neck.

"So let me guess," he said, "it's this last door. The pool is right outside there, isn't it?"

"And my bed is right inside here."

It all came clear to her as he bore her across the threshold of her bedroom. She understood perfectly why she had put clean sheets on the bed before she made it and pulled back one corner; why she had shaved her legs and washed her hair and put on her most flattering clothes, including a matching bra and panty set; why she had made coffee and sat anxiously by the door, just waiting for him to knock. She might not have had any expectations—she was no fool, but this was precisely what she had been hoping for.

Garrett laid her gently on the bed and, as he bent over, she took hold of his shoulders and pulled him down on top of her. They kissed, his mountainous erection pressed against her abdomen. When he raised up on his elbows, her hands went to the front of his shorts, loosening the belt and undoing the hasp. She pushed his shorts down over his hips as she watched. Instantly his penis straightened, gloriously firm, the end dripping with pearly cream.

He studied her face as she reached for his member and caressed it, milking a fat, glistening drop from it. Putting his hands beneath her, he lifted her and scooted her toward the head of the bed. Rising to his knees, he unfastened her Capris and slowly pulled them down over her hips, sliding her panties with them. He took the slacks off one leg, then the other, gazing down at her expectant vagina.

Wordlessly he lowered his face to her crotch. For an instant there was the strangest, most erotic sensation as he brushed the soft whiskers on his chin against her secret flesh, then she felt his tongue enter her passage, pressing upward maddeningly against her clitoris. Irresistibly she raised her hips toward him, spreading her legs further. She felt one of his hands on her tailbone, lifting her firmly against his face, while the other climbed to a breast, caressing the nipple.

Wendy heard herself moan, one note that lasted for seconds, testifying with undeniable clarity to the ecstasy she felt. "Ohhh."

He released her bottom and put his hand between her legs, a finger easing itself into her vagina beneath his tongue and resting on the thickening above her clit.

"Ah!" Her neck arched backward, her eyes closed. "Oh . . . god. . . . Oh . . . god."

He rubbed the spot firmly in rhythm with the motion of his tongue. To her surprise she came suddenly. A quiver ran through her, followed by a second and third. She felt her limbs collapsing as she relaxed, her body completely as ease, her eyes closed.

Wendy felt the sweet thrill of his firm body drawing next to her. He was moving up in the bed. When she opened her eyes, he was looking into them. Her hand drifted down to his cock, still wooden and bowed.

"Make love to me. . . . Come in me."

A gradual smile spread across his face. "It would be my great pleasure."

Without taking her eyes from his, she widened her legs and felt him move between them. The weight of his chest descended to her and his back arched and then came the slow, deep penetration. For a time he did not move. She marveled at the wetness of her passage. She could not remember having been so aroused. And when Garrett began rock back and forth, she felt the movement throughout the core of her body. Her nipples had a rawness, a tenderness to them, even though they were like stalks as his chest slid to and fro against them. For several minutes, glorious minutes of pure sensation, they made love without speaking. And suddenly with almost no foreshadowing, she came again.

"Ah! Ah! . . . Ah! . . . Ah! . . . Garrett."

He answered, his breathing labored. "Yes?"

"Garrett."

". . . Yes."

His voice seemed distracted, troubled and she realized he too was about to climax. Once again the idea of coupling with this wildly attractive man sent a thrill through her and Wendy's body did what it had never done, as she came again, a profound, consuming orgasm.

Garrett came, forcing himself deeply into her, clinging tightly to her. Though his rhythmic movement had ceased, she felt his cock throb within her, pulsing again and again. Gently he lay against her, his breath hot on her neck. Wendy slipped her arms around his chest and looped her legs around his behind, pressing him against her, holding him inside her.

A full minute passed as his breathing slowed and neither spoke. For some reason—some feeling she could not express in words—she was overcome with melancholy and joy and she began to cry, even to give some quiet, tiny sobs.

Garrett raised up and looked at her in dismay. "Wendy, did I hurt you?"

She sniffed. "No. . . . No, Garrett. . . . You made love to me. You really made love to me. Beautiful love. . . . Unforgettable love."

He rolled onto his side, watching her, filled with curiosity.

"I have to ask you a question," she said.

"Okay."

"Two questions."

He smiled. "Okay."

"Or more maybe. First—and I'm not sure how to ask this—was that, you know, normal?"

"What?"

"The way we made love. Is that usually, you know, what happens when you make love?"

He sighed and looked down. "Well. I have to admit that you got me a little worked up there, you know. Plus, I'm a little out of practice. Usually I can go like two or three times that long without popping. But making love to you is, well . . . it's pretty exciting and I guess I did come a little quicker than I wanted."

She stared at him. "You mean to tell me that usually you can fuck twice that long without coming?"

He nodded. "At least."

She closed her eyes. "Oh god. I have died and gone to heaven." She drew a deep breath. "Mr. Garrett Bolden, I have to confess that I just set a kind of a strange record just now."

"Yeah?"

"Yeah. I came three times." She watched his face to see his reaction. "Three times. In my whole life I never came three times. I mean, three times in one . . . one session of having sex." She thought about it. "Oh hell. I never came three times in one weekend. I never even came three times with my vibrator. I guess I didn't feel like I deserved to come more than once, you know?"

He stared at her, his head propped on his palm. Softly he said, "May I tell you how beautiful you are?"

". . . What?"

"You are such a lovely person. Lovely in every way. Sitting at the table this morning, looking at you without you having had a chance to put on makeup or brush your hair, you were so very pretty. And as I watched you ever since—clothes on and clothes off—everything about you is just so finely drawn, like a portrait painted by an artist who loves his subject. The shape of your face, your long legs, your fingers, your smooth skin, the flavor of your flower—"

She giggled.

"Your hips and your breasts. Your touch. Everything about you is so beautiful."

"Well," she said, a voice sheepish, "my friend Laura did comment on my girls."

"Oh?"

28

"Yes. She said I have 'classic tits.'"

He laughed. "And to what degree has she actually seen them? I mean, in the flesh or just covered up?"

"Oh. Well she comes over to swim during the summer. She's seen me in a bathing suit."

"Yeah? Well you can tell your friend Laura for me that no bathing suit in the world can do justice to your girls in the flesh."

She blushed and pulled her arms over her breasts. "Oh my god! Oh my god! My nipples are getting hard. We have to stop talking about them. They're self-conscious."

"Okay. Then let's talk about the perfect curvature of your bottom."

"Oh. . . . Oh." She reached for him, caressing his stubbly check with her fingers. "You're so wonderful. . . . And that brings me to question number two."

"Shoot."

"Can we do this again?"

"Um." He raised up, looking around the bedroom for a clock. "I would love that, but I'm not sure we have enough before Trouble One and Trouble Two get home."

"No, I know that. . . . I mean, will we do this again? Will you make love to me again?"

His expression was one of uncertainty. "I'm so glad you asked me that question. Do you want to make love to me again?"

"Oh absolutely."

"Well, good. You see, while we were having sex there, at the back of my mind was this worry that you were just rebounding, you know. That you were trying to see, now that you're divorced, what it was like to do it with somebody new." He studied her face. "I was so afraid you wouldn't want me after this."

An incredulous smile slipped through, though she held back a laugh. "So you're saying you were afraid I wouldn't respect you in the morning?"

"Oh my god. Yeah. I guess that was it. Exactly."

She pinched his ear lobe with her thumb and index finger. "I hope you can trust me on this, Garrett. You're not just a one-time afternoon delight for a high-society woman like me. I promise I would never take advantage of you like that."

He seemed to be choosing his words carefully. "You can prove it by setting another time for us to get together."

"Well . . . what's today?"

"Tuesday."

"Okay. How about either Friday night or Saturday. Or Sunday. Aaron—my ex—has the girls this weekend. He gets them from Friday evening until Sunday night and I have no plans."

"Well then, how about Friday night?"

"Okay."

"How about Saturday?"

She giggled. "Okay."

"And, let's go for the hat trick, how about Sunday?"

"Okay. What's a hat trick?"

"Oh. That's in hockey when the same person scores three goals in one game."

". . . Honey, you can score as many times as you want."

He dropped onto his back, looking up at the ceiling. "So, hey. What time does your ex pick up the girls on Friday?"

"Usually about 5:30 or 6. There's no set time. Why?"

"Well—thinking about how crazy your daughter is about Mads—he has a triangular on Friday afternoon. Maybe you and your girls would like to go."

"What's a triangular?"

"Oh. That's when three schools have a competition. This is a triangular swim meet at the Central Natatorium. Mads will be swimming in at least four events. It starts at 4. If you meet me at the door about 3:50, I can get us in for free."

"Wow. A free, up-close and personal view of Mads. Tina

will love you as much as I do." Instantly she regretted her words. "I mean—"

"I know what you meant."

"How long will it last?"

"Couple hours, probably."

"So is it okay with you if I have the girls' dad pick them up there when it's over?"

"Sure."

". . . So, I have another question. You said you would have Mads become the one who services our pool?"

"Yeah?" He rolled onto his side, facing her.

"Well . . . knowing how crazy my thirteen-year-old is about him, do you think I should make sure I'm here and keeping an eye on things when he's here?"

Garrett laughed aloud. "Uh, no. You have absolutely nothing to worry about."

"Well," she said, "I know Mads is a great guy and everything and Tina is just a skinny kid, but she would seriously do anything he asks her. He's like a god to her."

"Trust me on this. You have nothing to worry about."

She studied his face. "'Cause he's got a smoking hot girlfriend?"

He leaned toward her. "'Cause he's gay."

". . . Gay?"

He nodded. "Last summer one of my well-heeled customers had a seventeen-year-old daughter who pretty much creamed every time Mads came over to clean her pool. She tried and tried to get him to notice her. Finally she had her father contact me to ask Mads if he would be willing to be her escort to some society thing for rich young ladies."

"A debutant ball?"

"If you say so. Anyway, this guy was going to rent Mads a tux and have him arrive in a limousine to pick up his girl. I thought, 'Shit, he can't pass this up.' So I dropped it on Mads and he hems and haws and says, 'Gee—'"

"'Gee'?"

"That's what my guys call me. He says, 'Gee, I got something to tell you. I'm gay.' I said, 'You're gay?' He says, 'Yeah. Queer as a two-dollar bill.' And I said, 'So gay you're going to turn down a ride in a limo and a banquet and fitted tuxedo?' He says, 'I have zero interest in that.' So I went back to the customer and told him Mads was in a committed relationship."

She turned it over in her mind. "So Marshall Madison is gay."

"Yep."

She gazed at him. "If it's okay, can we just not tell Tina?"

"I won't tell Tina that Mads is gay if you won't tell her that I had splendid mad sex with her mother and I can't wait until Friday night to do it again."

32

Chapter Three

Garrett was leaning against the brick wall by the front doors of the natatorium watching her as Wendy led her little troop up the sidewalk. She wondered what impression the three of them made as they trekked toward him: Tasha in the back, her jaw set, tablet computer pressed to her side; Tina in the middle, wearing the perpetual put-upon, bored look of an early adolescent; and herself in the front trying not to show the ecstatic anticipation she was feeling at seeing this man again.

They had spoken only twice on the phone after their encounter in her bedroom, brief necessary conversations to verify the details of this event—and for her to tell him that this was to be a surprise for Tina. It had seemed to her while they were speaking that each had a longing to talk but also a feeling of uncertainty. Perhaps each wondered how they could build upon the amazing time of intimacy—physical but also emotional—they had shared. And, too, she wondered if he harbored reluctance about seeing her again, if after they had parted he had regretted setting this date.

She heard Tina gasp when they were about twenty feet from the entrance. "Oh my god," she whispered, "isn't that Mr. Pool Man."

"Yes, dear, that is Mr. Bolden. His company does service our pools."

"He saw my underwear."

"You have all your clothes on, dear. I predict he won't mention it if you don't."

"Hi," Garrett called. "It's good to see you ladies." He held the door open. "Thank you so much for accepting my invitation."

"Hello, Garrett." Wendy could not keep the charmed smile from her face. "Thank you for inviting us. So this is a triangle?"

33

"Uh. It's a triangular. There are three teams competing against one another in a swim meet." He glanced at Tina as he led them through the lobby to the pool area. "Your mom told me you were into competitive swimming and I heard that this meet was taking place. Since these swimmers are older than you, I thought you might pick up a few pointers."

"I hate swimming!" Tasha called from behind them.

"Oh?" Garrett responded. "I guess that big pool in your backyard is wasted on you."

"No," she corrected, "I like swimming in the pool. I hate going to all these races."

"I know that, dear," Wendy answered. "That's why I told you to bring something to read."

"Your name is Tasha, right?"

"Yeah. So?"

"You know what I heard about those computer tablets," he asked.

"What?"

"I heard they are so advanced now you can throw them into the water and they'll still work."

"No!" she cried in alarm, pulling the tablet close to her body.

Garrett shrugged. "I guess we'll never know."

Wendy leaned close to him. "You are bad."

Tina studied the surroundings as they walked into the cavernous pool area and were greeted instantly by the odor of chlorine. She seemed surprised to see only a few dozen spectators. The meets she had attended the previous year were viewed by hundreds. There were, however, photographers and reporters with name badges around their necks. They stood around the edges of the pool in various place.

"What schools are these, exactly?" she asked.

Garrett produced several programs and handed one to the girl. "Well two them I don't know. One is Woodcrest Academy. One is Buena Vista Prep. . . . And the other is Glades High."

34

She caught her breath. "Glades High?"

"Yeah. That's what it says here."

She looked at her mother. "Doesn't Mads swim for Glades High?"

"I think so."

"Oh my god! You mean Mads is going to swim here today."

Garrett pointed to an empty section of bleachers close to the start-finish. "These are some good seats. Real close. We should be able to see the action pretty well."

An air of awe had descended upon Tina, who stood looking at the gaggle of athletes gathering near the massive digital timing clock. When Wendy touched her arm to have her follow them up the aluminum steps, she didn't move. Finally, glancing away from the swimmers only briefly, she climbed the few steps and sat down beside Tasha, her mouth open. She opened the program and studied it furiously.

"The events don't start for about ten minutes, dear," Wendy said. When Tina did not react, she continued, "You know, Mr. Bolden knows Mads personally."

There was the familiar little gasp. She looked at Garrett with new appreciation.

"You do?"

He nodded. "I was his swim coach when he was about Tasha's age."

Tasha eyed him suspiciously for an instant.

"Of course, he was a lot nicer than Tasha."

"Everybody's a lot nicer than Tasha," Tina said. "Was he always a good swimmer?"

"Oh yes. With Mads it was a matter of teaching him, you know, turns and pacing and when to breathe."

"When your head is out of the water," Tasha quipped.

"I can't believe you actually know Mads." She looked back to the program. "Is he swimming in all these?"

"Well, not all the events," he said. When she glanced back

at him he said, "I think Mads will probably swim in four or five events at most."

"That's all?"

"Probably," Garrett answered. "After all, these are three teams swimming against each other."

"But Mads could win every event. He could be like that Olympic guy who won all the golds."

"Well, the Olympic guy didn't have to swim all those events consecutively in one day. And, yes, Mads could win each event, but he can't swim them all in succession. Plus, there are rules in high school meets like this that prevent one swimmer from participating in all the events."

"Why?"

"Exactly so a guy like Mads can't dominate a meet singlehandedly. This is a team competition. The teams win or the teams lose and Mads is only one guy on the team."

Tina looked down at the program again. "Well who are these teams?"

Garrett leaned back against the bleacher seats behind him. "As I understand it, Buena Vista is a school from somewhere around Atlanta. And Woodcrest is from up in Virginia."

She looked at him skeptically. "Atlanta, Georgia?"

"Yep."

"Georgia and Virginia? Why are they coming all the way down here just for a triangular swim meet?"

He shrugged. "To swim against Mads."

"What?"

"Yeah. Glades has got the best swim team around here. Maybe in the whole state. They're good without Mads, but Mads makes them great. These other two schools are well known for having outstanding teams as well. . . . So the quality of the teams you're about to watch is far and away better than any of the teams you've seen before."

Uncertainty flashed across her face. "But he can still win, right? Can his team beat them?"

36

Garrett shrugged. "Why don't you ask him." He nodded toward the pool.

Wendy and Tina glanced toward the water in time to see Mads Madison, clad in his black-and-gold warm up suit, climb onto the stands and sit down beside Garrett. Tina gasped. From the corner of her eye, Wendy watched crimson streaks light up the girl's cheeks.

"Hey, Gee." The boy's voice was unexpectedly deep and rich.

"Mads, how you doing?" Garrett answered casually. "These are the folks I was telling you about. This is Ms. Wendy Marbury and her daughters Tina and Tasha."

"Hey."

Tina, her mouth open, did not speak. Tasha looked up from her tablet for only an instant.

His hands folded in front of him, Mads spoke to Tina. "Are you the one who's a competitive swimmer?"

Tina's gaze moved from the boy to her mother, who spoke up. "I believe he asked you a question, dear."

"Yes. I swim."

"So what strokes and distances do you swim?"

"Um. Um. . . . I do 100 and 200. Mostly freestyle and backstroke." She didn't look directly at him as she continued. "I tried the butterfly, but I got too tired."

"Yeah, it's wears me out too."

"So—so." She scooted forward, suddenly eager to talk to him. "What are you swimming today? How many races?"

He sighed and shrugged. "They only let us swim in four events. So coach has me in the 200 butterfly and individual medley and I'm anchoring a couple relays."

"Mr.—" She glanced at Garrett. Clearly she had forgotten his name.

"It's Gee," Mads said. "Everybody just calls him Gee."

"Well, Mr. Gee says these are really, really good teams you're racing today."

"Yeah they are. Like some prep schools recruit football and basketball players. These guys recruit swimmers."

"Well, is Glades going to win?"

Mads shook his head. "It'll be tough. I think we should do pretty well in the individual races, but the relays are going to be a test. I've been watching videos of these guys and comparing times. They have some real depth."

"Still you can win, right?"

"I hope so." As quickly as he had appeared, Mads got to his feet. "I got to get back over to the team."

"Hey," Garrett said. "Tasha had some advice that might help you."

The little girl looked up at the sound of her name.

"What's that?"

"She said only breathe when your face is out of the water."

The boy laughed, a hearty, genuine laugh. "I don't know if I'll be able to remember that in the middle of a race, but I'll try." He looked at Tina. "I guess I'll see you . . . what, a week from tomorrow?"

He turned and bounded down the bleachers.

"A week from tomorrow?" Tina asked. "What's a week from tomorrow? Is there another meet?"

"No, dear," Wendy replied. "Mads works on the weekends servicing swimming pools for Mr. Bolden. Mr. Bolden has assigned him to service our pool and his first time coming to our house is a week from tomorrow."

Her mouth dropped open. ". . . Mads Madison is coming to our house?"

"Is that a big deal?" Garrett asked.

"That's awesome."

"Well I don't know," he continued. "What if he gets his brains beat out today by these other swimmers. You may not want a loser to clean your pool."

"Don't be ridiculous. He's going to win every race."

"Oh, Really? I wish I could believe that, Tina." He face

was transformed with a wistful, playful look. "I'm just not sure Mads is up to this level of competition."

She turned to him, her voice indignant. "I'll bet you a banana split that Mads wins every race he's in today."

"Ha! You're on. And I want extra whipped cream and pecans on it."

Tasha glanced up at the mention of a banana split. "What about me?"

"I got a bet for you, Miss Mischief," Garrett said. "Know what it is?"

"What?"

"I bet a hot fudge sundae I can grab your arm and your leg and, from right here where I'm sitting, throw you like a Frisbee to the fourth lane out in the middle of the pool."

"No!" Her voice was defiant.

Garrett gave a dejected hiss. "Well I guess we'll never know. You probably wouldn't have paid off anyway."

He pulled his cellphone from the holder on his belt and leaned back. Wendy watched him from the corner of her eye. He seemed to be checking his messages, then responding to one.

She marveled at the obvious ease he felt around her daughters, the way he was able to tease them without being obnoxious. It was, she judged, his years of coaching children's swim teams that had taught him how to interact with such confidence and joy.

A tone sounded from her purse. She picked it up and fished her phone from an inner pocket. There was a text message from . . . Garrett Bolden. It caused her to start just a bit. Without looking at him, she opened the message and read.

Is it ok if I admire your magnificent girls right now? I mean the full grown tasty ones with the little bumps around the nipples, not T & T.

She resisted a smile and quickly entered: *Of course not, u naughty man. Eyes on the pool.*

In an instant another text popped up. *So it's not ok to stare at your perfect, smooth, luscious bottom either?*

No, Gee-Man.

Can I dream about your creamy delight?

She crossed her legs, straightened her back and tried not to think of his firm, naked body pressed against her in the bed. *Don't b awful. U R making me wet as the pool.*

His eyebrows arched as he read her reply and quickly he sent another message. *Really? Let me check?*

"Are you two texting each other?" Tasha asked curiously.

"What?" Wendy said.

"Does your mother know how to text?" Garrett responded. "I'm replying to some emails before the races start."

"And I, Miss Nosy," Wendy said with authority, "am reminding your father to pick you girls up here after the swim meet instead of at home."

Blissfully the loudspeaker came to life at that moment, welcoming the schools, spectators and press. The first race was announced.

Wendy deleted the text thread from Garrett, turned off her phone and dropped it back in her purse. She was surprised at the great sense of relief she felt. Obviously this man to whom she was so attracted was also interested in her. And he was playful. It was something she had not experienced in a male to whom she was attracted since . . . well, since before she began dating Aaron. It dawned on her with startling clarity that the father of her children had never really been playful.

The races began with a minimum of comments from the loudspeaker: an announcement of the distance, the strokes involved and the names of the swimmers. Wendy tried to understand what she was seeing, but apart from being able to tell who won each race, she did not understand the scoring or the arcane comments about the meet that passed back and forth between Tina and Garrett. She recognized quickly that he was sharing a depth of understanding about the meet strategy and the finer points of racing with her daughter, who obviously was quite receptive to what he explained.

Just before the beginning of the third or fourth race, she heard "Marshall Madison" announced and saw Mads standing on the starting platform at the head of one of the center lanes, shaking his arms and staring at the far end of the pool. The loud starting tone sounded and he sailed through the air into the water, disappearing and coming up half a body ahead of the other five swimmers. He was rotating his arms forward in the stroke Wendy knew was called the butterfly. He swam four lengths of the pool, finishing at least ten feet ahead of his closest competitor.

"That wasn't even close," Tina said.

"In this race, the clock was his competition," Garrett replied. "He's thinking ahead." When the girl looked at him, he continued. "He wanted to win convincingly, and also to see what he's going to be facing in the relays. He wants to have enough stamina left to achieve a certain time for his anchor legs in his upcoming races."

"What's an anchor leg?" Wendy asked.

Tina rolled her eyes. "Oh, Mom!"

Garrett turned to her. "The last person in a relay is called 'the anchor.' Usually that's the fastest swimmer, which on the Glades team is going to be Mads."

"Is his team going to win?"

He shrugged. "It's going to be really close. Glades was actually in third place before Mads won that and his teammate finished third. Now they are tied for first."

She was tempted to ask how he knew that, but did not want to endure the detailed explanation she would receive and, even more than that, Tina's scorn. Instead she nodded and watched swimmers taking their places for the next race. It was announced and begun with a claxon sound.

In a few minutes Mads came to the platform again and once again won his race handily. This had been what he called

41

a "medley," with him swimming a different stroke with each length of the pool—and with each lap his lead had increased. Garrett was right, she realized; regardless of who won the swim meet, the other two teams had come to compete against Mads.

Listening to the conversation between Tina and Garrett, Wendy began to understand that Glade kept sinking into second or third place and, each time Mads was in a race, they would draw even in the point count. After his third performance, a relay in which he had to come from ten feet behind at the beginning of his leg, Glade pulled into second place, ahead of the Georgia team by the narrowest of margins. Then there came a lull in activity as the swimmers rested for a few minutes. There was only race left, the medley relay.

Tina asked Garrett a question and he turned to her and replied. "It's real simple. Whoever wins this race wins the meet."

"Then Glades is going to win," she said breathlessly. "Mads is in this race."

He shook his head. "I hope so, but this isn't a sure thing, race girl. I've been paying attention to the different swimmers the two coaches have been putting into the different events. Each of teams has held their best athletes back for this race."

A look of confusion descended upon her. "What does that mean?"

"You remember Mads saying how deep the other teams were? That means the other teams could be very competitive in each event without necessarily using their best swimmers."

"So while Mads has been out there swimming his heart out, the other good swimmers have been resting?"

"Exactly."

". . . That's not fair."

He nodded. "Yeah it is. What if your team was up against a team that had one spectacular swimmer and in order to win you had to beat him in one particular race? It's just strategy."

She thought about it silently, then quietly said, "I still hope he wins."

Garrett nodded. "This is where his teammates have to help him, just like he's kept them in the meet."

"Hey. What's up?"

It was a man's voice—very familiar to Wendy and at the same time surprising. She turned to see her ex-husband, tall and lean, wearing a tie and long-sleeved dress shirt, sitting down on the aluminum bleachers beside her. A wave of wariness spread through her. She felt guilty about being somewhere in public with Garrett and having Aaron show up. The recognition that she was single and had no reason to feel guilty about anything came to her instantly as well, but it didn't wash away her anxiety.

"Are we late?" she asked. "I was just going to meet you on the parking lot."

"No. I'm just a few minutes early." He patted Tina on the head. "Hey girls. Is that Madison kid you're so crazy about swimming in this meet?"

The girl turned to face him. "Dad, this is the last event and Mads is the last swimmer," she said solemnly. "If he wins, his team will win the whole meet. But," she stressed, "he *has* to win."

Tasha looked up from the shining screen she held for an instant. "Dad—" She pointed to Garrett. "—that's Mr. Gee Bolden. He's really cool."

All three adults stared at her, each surprised for different reasons. Wendy was stunned at the child's pronouncement. She had no idea that Tasha thought so highly of this man she scarcely knew who had teased her so roundly. The two men faced one another and Garrett held out his hand.

"Hi. I'm Garrett Bolden."

"Aaron Toffler." Aaron studied his face. "Aren't you . . . Bolden Pools? Isn't that you're outfit?"

"Yes. That is me. And actually I've contracted with Ms.

Marbury to provide pool service for—" He searched for the right way to describe the man's ex-wife, children and former home. "—for her and the girls."

"Bolden Pools," Aaron said, cutting his eyes to Wendy. "You guys have quite the reputation. I'm a little surprised. Either Wendy has done very well with her famous budget or maybe I got suckered about her actual financial situation."

When Wendy's mouth drooped and she seemed at a loss to answer, Garrett spoke immediately. "I think this is a matter of priorities, Mr. Toffler. When you have a competitive swimmer with great potential like your daughter, you have to do whatever is necessary to give her the opportunity and edge she needs. Even if it means sacrifice."

Tina, a look of amazement on her face, turned toward Garrett slowly as he continued. "Of course, all Ms. Marbury has asked us to do is maintain the pool to a quality equal to the care you gave it. Which, by the way, was excellent."

A smile flashed across Aaron's face at the compliment. "Well, uh, thanks, Bolden. I appreciate that." He leaned forward, straightening the cuffs of his slacks. "Frankly I was mostly trying to keep the pool nice because I thought she was going to have to sell the house. Half of the equity is mine, you know."

"Oh?" Garrett said, innocently.

The loudspeaker sounded, announcing the ranks of the team in advance of the final race, then the swimmers from each team. The lithe athletes wearing black-and-gold suits were in the lane closest to the side where Wendy's group sat. Despite there being less than a hundred people present in the building, the feeling of excitement was electric and unavoidable.

"Come on Glades," Tina muttered, her thin, crossed legs bouncing on the bleacher.

The claxon sounded and the first set of swimmers flew into the water, splashed the length of the pool, turned and raced back to where the second set of teammates waited. Glades and the Georgia team each trailed the Virginia team by about ten feet. After the second set of swimmers, Glades was in second place by itself, though the Virginia team had increased its lead to fifteen feet. The third Glades swimmer closed the gap to seven or eight feet on his first length of the pool, but on the return trip he faded dramatically. As he approached Mads— waiting on the platform, shaking his arms—he was a dozen feet behind the Georgia school and twenty feet behind the Virginians.

Garrett shook his head warily. "He went out too fast. It's too big a lead."

Tina shook her head adamantly. "Mads can catch him."

Glades swimmer number three floundered more as he touched the wall, allowing the anchor swimmers for the other teams to gain another foot or two before Mads dove into the water. The Virginia swimmer, whom Mads had defeated in the butterfly race, pulled further away from the Georgia swimmer. Mads caught the lagging Georgia anchor by the time he finished one length of the pool. As Mads made his turn, the Virginian swam furiously, a dozen feet ahead.

On the final length of the pool, shouts and whistle filled the natatorium, belying the sparse crowd. Wendy marveled at the intensity around her. Everyone in the building was focused on the lead swimmer as Mads closed the gap between them with every rotation and kick. Thirty feet before the finish, Mads' shoulders were even with the Virginia swimmer's feet. Fifteen feet from the finish, Mads was a half body length behind. With shouts and splashes filling the air, the two seemed to hit the wall in the same instant. Wendy had no idea who won.

Tina leaped to her feet, clapping and shrieking in joy. "I told you! I told you!"

"Who won?" Wendy asked. "Who won?"

"Glades won," Garrett said calmly. "Look at the light

above lane three. One helluva good time too."

Tina collapsed onto the bleachers. "I knew he could do it. I knew he could."

"Damn," Aaron said quietly. "That kid is amazing."

"Can we go now?" Tasha asked, looking up from her tablet.

"In a minute, sweetheart," Wendy said. "Let's give Tina her moment here."

The little group sat watching the Glades swimmers celebrate. The three teams embraced. The announcer came over the loudspeaker and proclaimed the accumulated points for each of the teams. Glades High School had won.

Garrett stood and stretched. "They didn't charge you for a ticket, did they, Mr. Toffler?"

"Just call me Aaron. No. Since it was the last race, they just let me in."

"Well it was an exciting meet for sure." He turned to Wendy and the girls. "Good to see you folks. I'll make sure Mads gets rested up before he comes over to clean your pool."

An instant of panic flashed through Wendy. Weren't she and Garrett going to have a date?

"Uh, okay, Mr. Bolden," she said. "Thanks for getting us into the swim meet."

"I'm glad everyone enjoyed it, especially Tasha."

The younger girl, who had turned off the tablet, grimaced at him.

Stepping down from the aluminum bleachers, he reached into his pocket and produced his cell phone. Wendy immediately felt a wave of relief. As the girls followed their father toward the door, she reached into her purse and turned on her own phone.

She trailed her daughters to her minivan, listening as she walked for the reassuring tone of a text message. When she heard it, she couldn't resist a quick smile.

"So," she called to Aaron, "do you have big plans for the

46

girls this weekend? Or is it supposed to be a secret?"

"Ah, we've got a couple things to do," he replied. "We're going to have a great time, aren't we, girls. I'll have them back by suppertime on Sunday."

She opened the sliding side doors of the minivan and Tina and Tasha grabbed their backpacks and overnight bags. They seemed more resigned than excited.

"Goodbye. You two behave yourselves."

"Goodbye, Mom." Tasha gave her a hug and presented her cheek for a kiss.

Tina gave her a quick hug. "Bye."

Wendy watched them walk toward Aaron's new Audi. She opened the driver's door to her van and slide inside. Retrieving her cell, she saw a text from Garrett Bolden.

Call me when you can.

As she pressed the button, a feeling of relaxation and joy descended onto her. There was only one ring before he answered.

"Hello, Ms. Marbury. How are you?"

"I'm good. And how are you, Mr. Bolden?"

"I'm hungry. I was wondering if you might be willing to come to my house for supper."

"Sure. When?"

She heard him sigh. "Five minutes?"

She laughed. "I don't know where you live."

"It's easy to find. Seriously it's only five or ten minutes from where you are. I'll text you the address."

"Send it on. I'll be glad to come."

"I'm hoping for that too," he said, then hung up.

Instantly there was a tone and a text message with his address. There it was again, that marvelous adolescent thrill Garrett Bolden caused in her. She felt it in her chest, her arms, her legs and her crotch. As she started the van, her memory flashed to his lean, bare chest sliding maddeningly against her breasts.

The townhouses where he lived were set back from the road by one hundred yards or so. She drove by them two or three times a week and had never noticed them. She parked beside the truck emblazoned "Bolden Pool Service" and climbed the half dozen steps to his front door. When she rang the bell, she heard the brief of bark a dog.

Garrett opened the door and held it wide.

She looked around him. "You have a dog?"

"Ah yes. I should have asked you about that. How are you with dogs?"

"I love dogs. . . . Where is it?"

He called over his shoulder. "Spin. Come here. Meet Wendy."

A medium sized yellow Labrador appeared and sat down in front of her. She bent down and presented her hand and, after the lab had sniffed and licked it, she began to pet him.

"What a well-behaved dog."

"What a spoiled dog, you mean."

"His name is 'Spin.' Because he chases his tail?"

"No. It's short for 'spinnaker.'"

"Spinnaker. Is that part of a boat?"

He closed the door and led her through the spacious great room toward the open kitchen. "It's a sail. Whenever you are running—that is, when you are sailing and the wind is at your back—you can open this big sail that looks kind of like a parachute. It's called a spinnaker."

"Does your dog sail with you?"

He used a corkscrew to open a bottle of white wine. "Sometimes. During the week especially." He poured two glasses. "When I'm sailing on lakes. . . . Not so much when I'm on the big pond."

She took a glass from it and let the thick, woody aroma caress her noise. "The big pond? You mean the ocean? He doesn't like salt water?"

"No. He loves all water. He hates life preservers." He

48

touched the lip of his glass to hers. "The minute I put one on him, he commences to chewing it up. I can't keep one on him."

She sipped the wine, rich and full. "What difference does that make about where you sail?"

"Well, if I'm sailing on a lake and he falls off or—like a fool—he jumps off if he sees something in the water, he'll swim to whatever shore he sees. Or at least he can tread water until I turn around and get back to him. Out in the ocean the water can be a lot rougher and it can be hellaciously difficult to get back to him. And there is no shore he can see to swim toward." Garrett drank from his glass. "You have a dog?"

"We had a dog. Minute was her name. A little terrier mix. Our neighbor gave her the name when we got her. She said she was no bigger than a minute." She took a long drink. "She got cancer and died. The girls wanted another dog, but their dad wouldn't go for it." She finished the wine. "I don't know why. He was never the one who took care of her."

"Well," Garrett said, refilling her glass, "now you're free to get whatever dog you want."

She smiled at him slyly. "This is really good wine."

"Glad you like it. Not to light and not to tart. Chilled. . . . Just right."

"Are you trying to use these to liquor me up so you can have your way with me?"

He looked up to the ceiling, then down. "Well, I heard somewhere that all relationships are built on trust. So in respect of that, yes. I am definitely trying to liquor you up so I can take off all your clothes, kiss you all over and make passionate love to you."

She stared at him for a moment, then took another drink. "What's for dinner?"

"Italian casserole. Fixed it at lunchtime, but I just now put it in the oven. . . . So we have about forty-five minutes before it'll be ready."

"That's nice. Tour me."

"Oh. Okay."

She turned up her glass and took his and set both of them on the counter by the sink. She took his hand and led him out of the kitchen.

He motioned upward with his free hand. "This one room is my living room, dining room and den."

"Where is the bedroom?"

"Upstairs."

Holding his hand tightly, she started up the carpeted staircase. At the top of the stairs she led him into the first bedroom, dominated by a massive bed covered with a thick bedspread. She let go of his hand, kicked off her shoes and climbed onto the bed and lay at the very center.

He smiled wryly. "Man, that wine works fast."

"I've been waiting for you for about fifteen years."

". . . Well, I'm not going to keep the lady waiting."

As she watched motionlessly, Garrett pulled his polo shirt over his head. He unlatched his belt and his khakis dropped to the floor. He slid his underwear down his hips.

Wendy got to her hands and knees and crawled to him. She reached up, putting her hand behind his head and pulling his face to hers. They kissed slowly, sweetly. As she forced her tongue into his mouth, her hand dropped to his penis, which unmistakably had started to grow firm. She fell backward onto the thick quilt.

He undid the button on the front of her capris, unzipped them and pulled them off her legs with one long, smooth motion. Pulling her knees toward him, his hand beneath her bottom, his mouth descended onto her panties at her crotch. Through the sheer fabric she felt the wet firmness of his tongue pressing against her labia. Planting her feet on the bed, she pushed up, allowing him to hook his fingers in her panties and slide them off. Then his mouth was on her vagina again, the inner slickness of her lips opening to his rough tongue.

"Ah!" She drew a breath.

50

He ran his tongue from side to side against her clitoris. She felt his hand creep up to the center of her back and loosen the clasp on her bra. Her breasts sagged, free and aroused, eager for his touch.

Garrett turned her lengthwise onto the bed and lay down beside her. He pulled off her blouse and the bra and kissed between her breasts and then the nipples. They kissed again. She held their faces together and widened her legs and pulled him onto her. Without his guiding it, his member found her vagina and slowly entered her. For a minute they lay pressed together, his engorged member fully within her, her inner walls firm against him.

Then he began to rock, slowly, back and forth, his cock nearly emerging only to slip deeply within. There was the sloppy, wet pounding sound that aroused her all the more. Their eyes open, they stared at each other for minutes as she felt the approaching, inevitable climax. And when she came there was a burst of air from her vagina. A shiver ran through her body and she clung to him, her finger digging into his shoulders and her legs wrapped around his thighs.

"Oh. Oh. Oh. . . . Oh."

He stopped moving, looking into her eyes.

She brushed his face, listening to his hurried breathing.

"Did you come?" she whispered.

He shook his head. "No."

"Then fuck me more."

Chapter Four

She was startled from the entirely pleasant relaxation of peaceful sleep by a movement beside her in the bed. Not the movement of a fifty-pound ten-year-old child—as on those occasional nights when Tasha had bad dreams and climbed into her bed—but the motion of a full-grown man. And she was suddenly wide awake, lying on her side, staring at a dresser and a wall that wasn't hers.

In the next instant the memory of where she was came back to her and she relaxed and breathed. And in the next second she rejoiced in the feeling of crisp sheets against her totally naked skin. When was the last time she had slept in the nude? She remembered as well the events of the night before and the gathering sense of freedom that had descended upon her as she let herself enjoy one new experience after another— drinking an entire bottle of wine, making love multiple times, deciding with no preparation to stay the night—and as her innate feelings of inhibition and caution melted away.

Garrett moved again, closing the distance between them until she felt his arm cross over her shoulder and pull her gently toward him. There was that thrill again, the one she hadn't felt since she was a curious teenage girl, and now felt in each successive encounter with this man. She realized he wanted to spoon and was intrigued by the way she was so aware and in tune with his desires with so little verbal communication. And then she felt the unmistakable firmness of his erection against the cheeks of her behind and realized what he wanted—something she wanted as well.

Wendy took his hand from her shoulder and guided it slowly to her crotch, still thick with the chalky residue of their last lovemaking in the middle of the night, and pressed his fingers against her clitoris. He caressed it tenderly, back and forth, side to side. Almost immediately it grew damp. Indeed she was amazed at how quickly her body responded to his touch, as if it possessed its own underlying desire. When was the last time she had made love in the morning? Maybe on her honeymoon with Aaron? She couldn't remember. She didn't even use her vibrator in the morning.

She rolled onto her back, gazing at his face. They kissed as he pulled himself onto her, her legs widening in welcome. He entered her gently with several tentative, preparatory thrusts. His member seemed rock hard to her. Had he been that hard the night before? She felt her back arch in response. Again there was the sensation that her body was taking over the process as she pressed her hips up against him. Her eyes closed, her head drooped to one side as she focused on his penis sliding rhythmically through her labia and deep within her passage. They continued wordlessly for minutes. And just as it seemed they could make love this way forever, a sudden urgency descended upon her. Her eyes open, her face on his, wearing an expression of alarm, she pressed her heels against his buttocks, trying to hold him within her as she came.

"Naw . . . Ah . . . Ah . . ." She collapsed limply against the sheets.

Garrett slowed but did not stop the pulse of his love making. "Good morning to you too," he whispered.

"Oh god. . . . What a way to wake up."

". . . Has anyone ever told you how gorgeous you are?"

"What?" She stared up at the man who continued his powerful, deliberate penetration. "Gorgeous? . . . Just woke up. No makeup. Haven't combed my hair or brushed my teeth. Buck naked. . . . Are you blind, Mr. Gee?"

He grinned broadly, then suddenly stopped moving. "Maybe it's my vantage point. I mean the view from up here is really beautiful. You should to try it."

With that, and making sure to keep his penis within her, he lay tight against her, gripped her shoulders and rolled onto his back in the middle of the bed so she was astride him. He put his hands on her behind and began to ease her hips back and forth,

Wendy caught her breath, thrilled at the new stimulation of his member sliding directly against her clit. She put her hands on his shoulders and leaned forward, rocking toward him, her breasts dancing madly, unrestrained. He arched his neck and took one breast in his hand and put his mouth over the other, his tongue pressing the nipple inward.

He pulled his mouth away for an instant and whispered, "So . . . how's the view from the top, young lady?"

"Oh god," she whimpered. "Oh. You've got to stop that."

"Is it hurting?"

". . . No," she replied, her voice worried, "it's making me crazy. I think I'm going to . . . explode maybe."

He lifted his pelvis in response and she shook her head and shoulders.

"That's just not fair. . . . You're trying to make me . . . come."

"Yes, you beautiful woman." He seemed completely serene. "That is the idea."

". . . I didn't know."

"Didn't know what?" There was just the slightest urgency in his voice now.

". . . Didn't know we could carry on a conversation . . . you know, while . . . we are making love."

"Oh yeah. Oh yeah." He closed his eyes and lifted his chin. Within her, his member seemed to grow even firmer. "You know you can do lots . . . while you're having sex. . . . In Florida . . . in January . . . everybody has sex doggy style."

". . . Doggy style?"

". . . Yeah. So both of you . . . can watch . . . the race."

She giggled and in the next instant she came, a riotous, explosive orgasm that racked her and made her limbs quiver. And Garrett came as well, his face contorted as if he were engaged in a massive exertion. Wendy felt his cock spasm within her. Their simultaneous climax went on for seconds until both seemed to lose all strength. She drooped forward onto his limp form. Still deep within her passage, the pressure of his engorged penis sent tiny charges through her clitoris, and she responded with involuntary quivers.

At length, completely at peace and in comfort lying atop him, their genitals awash in shared effluence, she said, "This is so decadent. And so fucking much fun."

She felt him smile and heard him respond. "I'm so glad you're having a good time."

Wendy put her hands together on his chest, making a resting place for her chin. "You know, the downside to starting the day with fantastic sex?"

"What's that?"

"Nothing I do for the rest of the day is going to measure up to the way I started."

A soft whining sound came from the hallway outside his bedroom door.

"Oh. Old Spin." He lifted her easily and placed her beside him. "'Scuse me, Wendy. I have to walk my dog."

She watched him as he hopped out of bed, his member dangling and still partially erect, and pulled on a t-shirt and shorts and headed out the bedroom door. He spoke lovingly to Spin, who fell in bedside him looking up expectantly. She listened as they went down the stairs and out the back door. Then she sighed and stretched and rolled onto her back.

"Honey," she said lazily, "in your whole life you never been fucked like this. I lost count of how many times you popped, you slut. . . . I didn't even know sex could be like this."

Doubling her pillow, she propped her head so she could study his bedroom. It was neat and masculine without being too manly. Clearly it showed the signs of a designer, someone who wanted it to be appreciated not only by the man who slept there, but also any woman who might see it.

Wendy pushed aside the bedclothes, stood stretching, then went into Garrett's bathroom. She had flushed the toilet and washed her hands and face before she heard the door open again. Garrett was still talking to Spin. Doors and cupboards opened on the lower level. She heard dry dog food being poured into a bowl. She dropped back onto the bed and covered herself with the sheet just as her lover appeared at the door.

"Now what were you saying?" he asked.

She frowned. "What was I saying?"

"You were saying that starting the day with hot sex means you just don't have that much to look forward to."

"Yeah. . . . Well, unless you wanted to make love again. Just saying."

He laughed and dropped onto the bed beside her, rolling onto his back. "Maybe that's what they mean when they talk about 'starting your day over as many times as you need to.'"

She slid her hand under his t-shirt, caressing his chest as he put his hands behind his head and closed his eyes. How appealing he was in that totally relaxed moment. There was nothing about this man that was not attractive to her.

"So I was scoping out your bedroom here," she said softly.

"Yeah?"

"Either you are also a designer or you had somebody with real talent do your appointments."

He laughed and shook his head. "Ah, Jeanna."

"Jeanna?"

"Yeah. . . . She is this forty-something, very attractive divorcee who is a member of the racing club."

"Racing club?"

"Yeah. Sailboat racing." He glanced at her. "You saw those regatta trophies on the hearth, right? I used to race sailboats."

"Uh hmm."

"Right after I separated from Sherry and got this place, Jeanna—who's a decorator—offered her services."

"I bet she did."

"Right and right." He smiled. "But I wanted to keep things on the up-and-up. I told her I'd love for her to decorate if she'd let me pay her."

". . . And?"

"So she came in and in just a couple days she took my old knick-knacks and assorted crap that needed to be thrown away and she made this place look really nice."

"And you paid her how?"

"Ha." He chuckled. "We weren't sexual. Not that she wasn't interested. She was. I'm pretty sure that's really the reason she wanted to decorate." He shrugged. "And she is a lovely and attractive person. . . . She's just not—I don't know—appealing to me."

Wendy studied his face. "Well, then, do you find me appealing?"

"Seriously? After Tuesday and last night and midnight and this morning, you can ask that?"

"Well . . . I just—"

"You just wonder what makes you special."

She shook her head. "I never said I was special."

"No, love. I'm saying you're special. Very special."

She stared at him. "In my whole life, no one ever said that to me."

He returned her gaze in silence, slowing reaching out and caressing her cheek with his fingertips. "Maybe they thought you already knew how special you are. In fact, I don't know how you could be unaware. It's abundantly obvious to everyone around you. . . . Well, maybe except for your ex. Nothing personal, but that guy seems a little oblivious to me."

Wendy chuckled. She covered his fingers with hers. "I'm—I'm nothing special, Garrett. I'm just me."

His expression clouded. "Let me spell this out for you,

Wendy. Because even exceptionally bright people—like yourself—can sometimes be unaware of what's obvious to everyone around them." He paused, his eyes fixed on hers. "First of all you are special in outward ways the world can see. You are a self-supporting professional woman and mother. Just listening to you discuss your budget, I could tell you know your way around finances. Anybody can see that. And anyone who is interested can see that you have dealt very well with your children and your ex-husband through the process of divorce. You managed to be able to stand up for yourself, to not interfere between him and your daughters and you can be around him without expressing a lot of negative emotions."

She smiled. "You mean like rage, disdain, disgust, contempt . . . ?"

"Yeah. Like those." His look became more intense. "But those are just the special things the world can see. . . . More than that you have the ability to bring joy to the people around you. Clearly you are willing to make sacrifices for those you love. You have—I'm not sure what to call it—a quiet, undemonstrative insight. Like the way you picked up on the fact that I had a designer decorate my house. You seem quick to answer the needs of others, like your children. But you don't seem very demanding when it comes to your own desires." A bright smile flashed across his face. "And you are so incredibly beautiful. And sexy. And just so much fun."

Wendy had to look away from him. She knew she was blushing. "Okay. Thank you for saying those nice things—"

He cut her off. "You don't believe me, then?"

"Well it's not—I mean, I would like to believe what you said about me, but—"

"Name one thing I said that isn't true."

Silently she went back over the list of compliments he had given her. She remembered them all. Yes, she could see the basis for everything he had said.

"You see?" He nodded slowly. "You have to admit it. You

are special." And when she still couldn't respond he continued. "That's not to say you aren't also mysterious to me in a lot of ways."

"Mysterious?" she responded skeptically. "Be real, Mr. Garrett Bolden. You know me at great depth."

They laughed.

"What I mean is," he said, "I don't know your heart's deepest desires. It's because you suborn them to the desires of others. What do you wish you could do just for yourself?"

An image of the two of them—making love, climaxing together, lying in each other's arms—flashed through her mind. Her lips parted, but she did not speak.

"You know what, Wendy? I bet you don't even know yourself what you most want in this life. I bet you've never allowed yourself to dream about what would make you happy, regardless of what anyone else wants." He fell onto his back, staring up at the ceiling. "So what are you doing today? And tomorrow?"

"Today? Uh. Well. I'm just going to clean around the house. Maybe watch some movies. I'm pretty much caught up on my number crunching."

He turned his head toward her. "Ever been to Savannah?"

"Savannah? Georgia?" She shook her head. "No."

"Want to go?"

"What?"

"I have a job there this weekend. There is this high-rise hotel called the Spaniard's Revenge. They have two indoor pools: a floor level pool and an executive pool about twelve stories up. Periodically the circulation system of that upper pool goes haywire and they don't seem to have anybody in Savannah who can fix it. So they call me."

"Well . . . well."

"Well?"

"How—uh—how long will it take? I have to be home when Aaron brings the girls back at 5 tomorrow."

"It's right at a four hour drive."

"Okay, and how long will it take you to fix the pool?"

He chuckled. "About an hour. They don't know that. They think it takes a full day. That's why they pay me $1000 every time I repair it?"

Her jaw dropped. "$1000?"

"Plus expenses. Plus they put me up in one of their suites."

"Well, uh. When would we leave?"

Garrett raised his head to look at the clock on his mantel. "It's almost seven."

"Seven? Seven a.m. is all? I made love before seven in the morning?"

"Yes, darling girl. If you want, I can follow you over to your house and we can leave your car there. If you're willing to eat breakfast while we drive, we can leave by eight a.m. and we can be in Savannah in time for lunch. Then we'll go to the hotel and I can have the upstairs pool up and running by two and we can spend the rest of the day and night enjoying the city. And each other. Then tomorrow morning—have you ever had shrimp and grits for breakfast?"

"No, actually. I like seafood though."

"It's a real low-country treat. We can have breakfast and maybe lunch there and still be back here by five."

A strange feeling was descending upon Wendy. It was the sensation of joy and freedom and fulfillment unlike anything she had ever experienced before, and with it was the built-in caution she had acquired over all the years. Being with Garrett, the idea of spending more time simply enjoying her life with him seemed almost too good to be true. The only way to find out, she thought, was to go ahead and dive into the deep end to see.

"So . . . what kind of clothes should I take?"

She woke and realized she had been lying against his shoulder as she slept. Garrett had turned the front seat of his

60

truck into a bench seat so she could sit beside him as they rode. Half an hour after she finished her bagel and coffee, sitting close beside him in silence, she had fallen asleep. And now she had no idea how long she had been sleeping or where they were.

"How long was I asleep?"

"Thirty hours. I finished fixing the pool and we're on our way back to Orlando."

She laughed and sat up. "I wasn't that tired. I don't even know why I got sleepy."

"I'm pretty sure it was staying up all night making love. Or it could have been the drugs I put in your wine."

"You drank that wine too."

"Yeah. I thought it was only fair for you to have your way with me."

"Right. It worked. So how far are we from Savannah?"

He shrugged. "We're still a couple hours out. Let me know if you need to stop."

"Okay."

Wendy stared down the interstate. She tried to focus on the road signs or the traffic on the opposite side coming toward them. Or the great volumes of Spanish moss hanging from the trees along the highway. What was she feeling?

A strange restlessness descended upon her. It wasn't hunger or fatigue. It wasn't anxiety or anger. What was she feeling?

Without looking at Garrett, she scooted to him. She put her hands on either side of her slacks and slid them down below her hips. He glanced at her curiously as she did. Then she pushed her panties down as well. She took his right hand and gripped his first and middle fingers and pulled them down across her naked abdomen. Garrett was startled, but did not resist. Wordlessly she began to slid his fingers against her clitoris. Momentarily, as the lips of her labia grew wet, she forced his middle finger inward, moving it in and out.

Garrett stared down the road, a smile spreading across his face.

Wendy continued to work his fingers against her clit. She found herself squeezing her breasts between her arms, her nipples erect within her bra. Closing her eyes, her head forward, she moved his hand back and forth against her sex. As she felt the orgasm approaching, she pressed her thighs against his hand, holding it in place against and within her vagina.

"Oh, oh, oh, oh, oh . . . oh." She relaxed, still holding his hand within her taut legs, waiting for her breathing to calm. She glanced at him. "That's the first time in my life I have ever done anything remotely like that. . . . Thank you, Mr. Bolden."

He looked at her. "That was your first time? My first time too. . . . I got to hand it to you."

She giggled girlishly. "I'm not sure you're a good influence on me, you know."

"Me? That was my responsibility? Are you saying I initiated that?"

She nodded. "Yes, you did, Mr. Testosterone—sitting over there driving like a hunky, dreamy dildo. A week ago I was a chaste, modest, single mom living a normal, non-horny life. Then I met Mr. Garett Bolden. Now I have hot, wet sex at all hours. My body makes noises when I come that it never made before and I use my boyfriend's hand to masturbate myself." She turned to him with an anxious look. "You my boyfriend, right?"

"I sure to god hope so."

Wendy might have seen larger hotels in her life, but never one as opulent and luxurious as the Spaniard's Revenge. Garrett had driven past the valet stand, waving at the fellows who waved back in recognition, and parked near a service entrance in a space marked "Employees Only." He picked up her overnight bag and his own, slinging them over one shoulder, and grabbed a tool kit in another canvas bag with his free hand and walked through a nondescript door.

"We can go through here to the main desk," he said. "I just need to get the key and talk to the manager for a minute."

She followed him through the maze of narrow corridors and wide hallways. When they came to the foyer, Garrett stepped aside, speaking with a sharply attired group of men who obviously knew him. Wendy stood and stared around the lobby area, trying not to allow her jaw to drop open in amazement. Everything she could see spoke of wealth. It was not gaudy or pretentious. Rather the furniture, window treatments and decorations were seamlessly elegant and in perfect condition.

"We're this way," Garrett said to her softly as he led her back down a hallway and to a set of service elevators.

After the doors rolled open and they were riding up to floor twelve by themselves, he turned to her. "Well, what do you think so far?"

A great smile broke across her face. "I have never been in a hotel this ritzy. Everything just takes my breath away."

"Good. We're in suite 1207, Wendy. As soon as we get into the room—if it's okay with you—I'll go over and fix the circulation system. I'm guessing it will take me the better part of an hour. When I get through, we can spend the rest of the day exploring Savannah."

"Works for me."

The door to their suite opened to a living room almost as large as her own great room. It was decorated in spotless contemporary furniture with actual oil paintings adorning the walls, and there was a half bath discretely placed near the bay windows. When she pushed back curtains, she found herself gazing onto the harbor and ocean. As she caught her breath, it dawned on her why some vistas were described as "breathtaking."

"Come check out the bedroom," Garrett called.

She walked toward the sound of his voice and found herself in a room almost as large as the living area and equally well-appointed. Dominating the elegant furnishings, decorations and large flat screen television was the king size bed, awash in pillows and dressed with the thickest bedspread she had ever seen.

"Nice?" he asked.

She nodded. "I guess this will do."

They looked at each other and broke into laughter.

"I hate to go off and leave you now, young lady, but duty calls."

"I'll be right here where you left me, Mr. Bolden."

He smiled and held up a card. "Here is the extra key if you get to feeling bored and cooped up and want to leave the room." He dropped it on the dresser, picked up his tool kit, smiled at her again and went out through the living room.

As she listened to the outer door latch and sat slowly on one of the padded arm chairs that faced the bay window, the surreal nature of all that had happened to her in the past week flooded her mind. After lengthy, anticlimactic months of struggling with Aaron, comforting her daughters and finally negotiating a mutually acceptable—if Spartan—divorce settlement, Wendy had anticipated a long period of adjustment. She would have to pinch pennies, fight depression, delay any sort of personal gratification and keep focused on the long term, she had assumed. Only now, less than seven days after the divorce decree was final, she was enjoying her life more than she ever had—and this weekend she was able to indulge in luxuries beyond anything she had ever experienced. Either she was hallucinating or she was truly having the—totally unexpected—time of her life.

Now the time had come for her to share everything with her best friend. She got up and fished her cell phone from her purse and, dropping backwards onto the great bed, she hit the button.

It was as if Laura had been holding her phone to her ear, waiting for the call. "Hello?"

"Hey, it's me."

"I know it's you. Where are you and who are you with?"

Wendy propped herself on her elbows. "Why? Is something wrong?"

"Aaron is looking for you?"

"What's up? The girls okay?"

"The girls are fine. Aaron figured out you weren't home last night. And you're not home today."

"And you know that because—"

"Because he called me to ask if I knew where you were. And he mentioned your Bolden pool man."

"Wow. That's really none of his business." She reflected momentarily over all her friend had said. "Are you telling me Aaron is jealous?"

"Ha. Yeah. I guess I am. Aaron Toffler apparently just realized what he gave up. How do you feel about that?"

Wendy collapsed back on the wonderful bed. "Talk about a day late and a dollar short. . . . Want to know what I've been doing?"

Laura took a quick breath. "What? Tell me."

"I've been having sex, like three times a day."

"Oh my . . ."

"And when I say sex . . ."

"Yes?"

"Well, I had no idea there was such a thing multiple climaxes."

"Oooo. . . Tell me. Is it the pool man?"

"Oh my god. Garrett Bolden. Yes, he is the man! My god is he the man. He stays hard forever. And when he finally, you know, when he finally does, it makes me pop again."

"Oh my god."

"And! He has a very smart tongue."

". . . Yes?"

"And he says . . ."

"Yes?"

"He says I taste like heavy cream."

"Oh god. . . . And you do him too, with your mouth I mean. . . . You do, don't you?"

". . . Well—"

"Oh yes! I know you do. How did Miss Chastity suddenly get to be Lady Horny-Beyond-Words?"

"I don't know. I don't know." She thrashed on the bed. "He just brings it out in me. And then he puts it in me and I can't help myself. The real question is, where has he been all my life?"

"Waiting for you to get unmarried, girl. So, where were you last night when Aaron drove by looking for you?"

"I was at Garrett's house. I went over for dinner and accidentally fucked his brains out and spent the night."

Laura laughed hard. When she caught her breath, she said, "You accidentally fucked his brains out? And are you there today? Aaron says your car is at your house today, but you aren't home."

"We took my car home from Garrett's place this morning before we left town. Why didn't he just call me, the old fart, if he wanted so bad to know where I was?"

"I'm sure he figured you wouldn't tell him."

"I would've told him it's none of his damn business."

"But it's my business though, hon. Where are you? I have to know."

She drew a deep, satisfying breath. "I am in Savannah."

"Savannah? Georgia?"

"That's right. I'm in a luxury suite of the Spaniard's Revenge Hotel lying on a king size bed, the top six inches of which is bedspread."

". . . You little slut. And you're going to have sex in that bed?"

"You bet your skinny ass I am."

"What made you choose Savannah? It's not like we don't have hotels in Florida that aren't 300 miles away."

"Garrett's working. That's why we're here. He's fixing one of the pools for the hotel. And in return they told him to bring his favorite sex object to copulate with in their hotter-than-honeymoon suite."

"You are such a shit," Laura said deliberately. "You know you have to be back by five tomorrow, right?"

"You like Tina and Tasha, right?" Wendy asked. When her friend gasped, she said, "Oh we'll be back. No erection lasts forever."

Laura's voice was tentative. "So this is pretty hot and heavy between you two. You think this is making up for all the lost love making you missed out on with Aaron?"

"You know, sweetie, I guess the time is going to come sooner or later when I'm going to get introspective about all this and maybe I'll decide this was nothing but rebound sex and I ought to hate myself and Garrett. Frankly though, in the meantime, I'm just going to keep right on popping."

"Oh, you naughty thing."

"Yes I am. . . . And you want to hear the most decadent thing of all?"

"Tell me."

"So I fell asleep next to Garrett this morning while were driving to Savannah."

"Yeah?"

"When I woke up, I was feeling really restless. Finally I realized I was just super horny. I wanted more of the sex we had all night and early this morning."

"Oh no. You're just like a teenager."

"That's not the good part. I don't know what I was thinking—that's just it, I wasn't thinking. My body and my desires just took over. Sitting there beside him, I just pushed down my slacks and my panties . . . ."

". . . Yes?"

"And I took his hand in my hand and . . . I made him finger fuck me."

Laura gasped, then giggled. "You did not. You decadent bimbo."

"I did. And I popped too. All over his fingers. Right there on the interstate."

Her friend seemed to be considering all she had heard. "Is this pool guy giving you drugs of some kind?"

"Yep. Regular testosterone injections. Administered internally with a long, blunt instrument. And sometimes orally."

"Wow," she said slowly, "I always thought you should break out of that shell Aaron kept you in, but I never in my wildest dreams you'd go off the deep end like this."

"That's it exactly!" she said excitedly.

"What?"

"That's just what I was thinking. There comes a time where you're not sure if the thing you see right in front of you is too good to be true or not. And sometimes, to find out, you just have to jump into the deep end."

"Well . . . I guess, if you're going to jump into the deep end—and you sure have—it pays to have a swimming pool man with you."

Wendy laughed. "So wait a minute. This is all about me. I haven't asked you what's going on with you this weekend?"

"Nothing. Nada. Not a single exciting thing. Although I am thinking about getting a swimming pool." After Wendy laughed, Laura continued. "Seriously though, I need to get off the phone. I'm need to have a chat with my vibrator."

Chapter Five

As she had on the long ride the day before, Wendy found herself scooting next to Garrett, leaning against his shoulder and falling asleep on the way home. This time when she woke, however, her mind drifted back to all that happened on their trip. Her eyes closed, her head pressed against him, she could not resist going back over the sweet, recent memories.

She had been waiting—naked, lying under the sheets of the great bed, her hands behind her head and a look of anticipation on her face—when Garrett came back into the suite after repairing the pool.

"I thought you said an hour," she had said, demurely.

"Uh, well, it's only been an hour and ten minutes. I had to go down and give some instructions to the maintenance guys. I guess I didn't take that into consideration."

"I just can't believe you kept me waiting."

A grin spread across his face. "So I guess I should cancel the carriage ride I booked."

"What?" She sat straight up, the sheets falling forward, revealing her breasts.

He laughed. "I'm just teasing. You don't have to book most carriage tours. You just show up. . . . And suddenly I'm not in such a hurry to stare at a horse's behind for the next hour." He gazed at her. "Did anyone ever tell you what splendid girls you have? That they are luscious? And tasty? And perfectly shaped? . . . And incredibly arousing?"

She gave the slightest giggle and her breasts danced for an instant.

"If I didn't know better, Ms. Marbury, I might think you were inviting me to join you in bed and make love." Her eyes opened round and wide. "Nothing gets by you, Mr. Bolden."

Without taking his eyes from her, he pulled his shirt over his head and unfastened and dropped his pants to the floor. She pushed back the bedspread and sheets and lay flat, her form completely bare. Her breathing, she noticed, had become quick and shallow.

Garrett came to her and they made love, wallowing in the bedclothes that somehow were both cool and warm at the same time. And, as she had each time they made love before, she climaxed multiple times, then held him inside her when at last he came. Tangled in each other's limbs, the silence broken only by their labored breathing, they lay for minutes in splendid, motionless, union; then slept.

They woke hungry and full of joyful eagerness. Garrett poured forth a list of possible places for them to visit, tours they could take, historical spots they could see—much, much more than they could possible take in during the hours that remained.

He led her down the back entrance to his truck and they fled off the parking lot toward the harbor. She was struck by his familiarity with Savannah and the pleasure he expressed in telling her about it as they drove along. He was childlike in his joy.

"You really like Savannah, don't you?" she asked.

"I do. And I like Charleston and Wilmington. Work takes me up there too sometimes. And south to Miami and Daytona."

"Are you this familiar with all those towns?"

"Pretty much. . . . Why do you ask?"

"Well. I don't know. I just seems like you're so excited to show this all to me."

He laughed. "Yeah. I guess I am." He thought about her words. "I guess I'm excited to have somebody with me I want to share this stuff with."

It surprised her. "You mean, I'm the first . . ."

"Yeah."

"Even after all those years—"

"Traveling. Seeing historical sites and enjoying local cultures. That just wasn't my ex-wife's thing." He glanced at her. "She liked staying home and drinking wine and watching those high-dollar home-makeover shows on TV."

"Oh."

"I'm not being critical of my ex," he said. "It's just that, you seem to enjoy getting out and riding around and experiencing different things in different places."

"I do. I really do."

"I'm glad of that. I just hope I'm not boring you."

She studied his profile and gradually began to smile. "Well, Garrett, over the last two days I have been horny, hungry, curious, intrigued and sleepy in that order. The one thing I have not been is bored."

"Oh. Okay then. Let's keep it rolling."

He drove along the outskirts of Savannah offering a continual travelogue of historical and architectural points of significance. Successfully maneuvering the full-size, extended-cab, long-bed truck into a parallel parking spot she would never have imagined he could have fit, he took her hand and led her to a carriage tour stand and pulled her onto a wagon that had just started to depart on its tour. He stuffed a green bill—she couldn't tell the denomination—into the pocket of the guide, who welcomed them and continued his dialogue with a happy smile.

She marveled as they rode along that she had never been on a carriage ride before. The clever commentary of the interpreter, the clopping sound of the horse's hooves and the gentle weight of Garrett's arm on her shoulder were almost hypnotic. Why had she never had an experience like this? Simple and innocuous as it was, this ride—like everything about this trip—was incredibly romantic. Why was she just living out this sweetness in her late 30s?

Near the end of the tour, he called out to the driver, who reined in the great work horse. Garrett discretely slipped him another bill and, taking Wendy by hand, stepped off the carriage onto the street.

"This will save us walking a couple blocks," he said. "There is a dessertery right here where we have to get a treat."

"I'm not sure I can handle any sweets," she protested.

"You always have to be ready for salted caramel chocolate. Or a banana split with three flavors of ice cream you never tasted. Or a chocolate volcano—"

"Oh my god! I gained three pounds just listening to you."

He stopped abruptly and turned back to her. "I need to bulk you up, sweetheart."

"You do?"

"Yep. Cause I have the secret intention of burning calories and this evening we're going to use up more calories than you have to spare."

She gazed at him and began to smile. "Sounds like it might be excruciating."

"Probably not. Probably it'll be exhilarating. With maybe a little exertion."

She followed him, mostly holding his hand, from the confection shop to the antebellum outdoor market to another carriage ride to a hole-in-the-wall café at supper time that served the most wonderful low country cuisine for supper. All too soon the late winter sky grew dusky and, as she realized the afternoon was gone, she found herself standing beside him as he opened the passenger's door of his truck.

She hesitated as she stood before the open door. "This has been such a wonderful trip. I can't tell you how much I have enjoyed this place. Especially being here with you."

"I'm really glad you're having a good time," he said slowly. "You sound as if you're ready to go home."

"No. Oh no. It's just, well, it's dark. Are we about to take in some night life?"

"Well." He squinted. "I had something in mind more just for the two of us."

"Oh. Okay."

She slid into the seat of the pickup. They drove the short distance back to the hotel in silence and he took her hand and led her through the service entrance.

As they rode up the employee's elevator, he turned to her and spoke. "So we're going to our floor, but not our room."

"What's on our floor besides the suites?"

He could not suppress his grin. "I'll show you."

They walked down the broad hallway and stopped before a door with a sign: "Upper Level Pool."

She stared in awe as he opened the door onto a room with a medium sized pool and great bay windows overlooking Savannah and the ocean. The last glimmering of daylight was giving way to the lights of the city that were coming on before them.

"God, this is so beautiful."

"You, uh, have a swimming pool, I know," he said. "I guess I've been assuming you liked the water as well."

"Of course I do. Tina gets her love of the water from me."

"Well let's go for a swim."

She turned to him. "Garrett, I didn't bring a suit."

"Neither did I."

"You mean . . . you want to go skinny dipping?"

"Yep. Unless you're scared of me seeing your birthday suit."

"You are already well-acquainted with my birthday suit. What if somebody comes in?"

"They won't. I told the hotel management that the pool wouldn't be ready for use until Sunday morning."

"Should we not be in it?"

"Ah, the pool is actually more than ready. It was ready the minute I fixed the circulation system this afternoon."

"Well why—"

"For us," he said simply. "So you and I could have this moment to swim naked and alone looking down on

73

Savannah." He began to undo the buttons on her blouse. "Unless you don't want to."

She stood watching him—feeling more awe than anything else—as he slipped off her blouse, then her bra and slid her slacks down her legs. He turned her around as if she were a child to remove her pants and sandals and languorously guide her panties down and over her feet.

"You know, I feel just ever so slightly ridiculous. Well . . . and maybe a little aroused." She turned to face him. "Now you."

She undressed him. They stood together holding one another, pressed against one another, kissing in the vast room, dimly lit by the evening lights of Savannah.

"So let's try the water," he whispered. "You want to? This is the five foot section. We can jump in here."

"How cold is it?"

He shook his head. "Not cold. Just a little warmer than room temperature. I'll check it."

In one motion Garrett turned to the water and dove in, the effortless dive of a long-time swimmer. She saw him for an instant as a dark shadow against the light-colored bottom of the pool swimming away, then he disappeared entirely.

Wendy stepped to the edge, brought her arms together before her and dove in. She was instantly amazed at the difference in the way the water felt against her when she was completely naked. Water sucked against her breasts as she coursed forward and tickled her between her legs. And it occurred to her that this—swimming in the nude—was another first time experience. She stood on the bottom of the pool, her head out of the water, and wiped her hair back. As she blinked away the water, the sight of nighttime Savannah glistened before her. She stared at it, entranced.

Suddenly she was rising up out of the water. Garrett had come up behind her beneath the surface and gripped her legs beneath her knees. As he stood, her behind folded down on his

74

shoulders and he flipped her backwards into the water. Sputtering and laughing, she broke the surface.

"You think I can't dunk you?" she called.

"Exactly," he responded. "I think you can't dunk me."

"We'll just see about that," she said, splashing water onto his face as she made her way to him.

Laughing boyishly, he caught her hands and held them apart so she could not reach the water. For an instant they stood face-to-face. In the darkness the shadows could not conceal the intensity—the joy—in his eyes. He kissed her. Her breasts caressed his chest as if they too were kissing him. She heard him sigh.

"Would you like to try the spa?" he asked.

"There's a spa?"

"Oh yeah. And we don't even have to get out of the water. You just step up into it."

He took her hand and led her caddy-cornered across the pool to the shallow end. There were indeed two tiled steps up into a round well with seats. As she sat down, he leaned over the control panel. Warm jets burst to life and noisy bubbles surrounded them. She leaned back, giggling.

"I don't know whether to feel overjoyed or guilty," she said. "I can't believe we're up here in the dark and we have this all to ourselves."

Garrett slid along the tile until his bare side was pressed against hers and nodded toward the great bay window. "It's a spectacular view, isn't it?" He glanced at her. "I guess it's only fitting that I'm with a spectacular girl."

She turned to him, her mouth open, unsure of what to say.

"You know," he continued, "I call this my 'Savannah Secret View.' In just about every city I work in, I've found at least one place like this where there is a to-die-for vista. And it's always the same in that, well, I say to myself, 'Here I am, looking at this magnificent scene, but I have no one to share it with.'" He brushed her cheek with his fingertips. "Now here I am, sharing it with you. . . . I guess you'd say this is a major moment of fulfillment for me."

Despite the picturesque scene before her, Wendy could not look away from the man who was pressed to her side. Beneath the foaming spring she looped her hand over his thigh and pressed their legs together.

"If I didn't know better," she said just loudly enough to be heard, "I might believe you are telling me all these lovely things to get into my panties. . . . Only, I'm not wearing any panties."

Garrett's expression seemed to soften. He held up a single index finger and said, "I have one more thing to show you."

He took her hand and stood and led her out of the water onto the carpeted landing around the pool. Before her, lit only by the lights of the city below and the emerging starlight, was a large chase lounge. It was obviously made for more than one person. Folded on it were thick, white towels.

"Try lying on this material. It's the neatest stuff ever. Even if you're wet, you can lie on it without getting cold. It's like a chamois for your body. . . . And you can dry off with one of these towels the hotel keeps up here for pool guests. They're thick and really big."

Gazing at the panorama below them, Wendy dried off and lay back on the lounge. It was richly padded, so much so she could not feel the supports beneath it.

"This is more comfortable than my own bed."

"I know, right?" he said. "They each cost a couple thousand dollars. I may ask for one in lieu of payment the next time they call me in a panic to fix their circulators." Making sure he did not interfere with her view, he sat beside her on the lounge.

Wendy rolled onto her side, gazing at the harbor and the stair-stepped buildings and the streets teaming with headlights. She felt him draw close behind her, looking above her and through the window, and heard him speak.

"This is so beautiful. I wish I had a painting of this."

"You can go get your phone and take a picture," she replied. "The ocean and the city aren't going anywhere."

He chuckled. "No, love. I'm not talking about Savannah and the Atlantic. . . . I'm talking about the image of you, lying naked, propped on your elbow, looking out the window."

His words caused that girlish thrill—the one she had begun to feel regularly now—to sail through her. She wanted to let the electric instant and the arousal that came with it to pass before she spoke, only she felt him press against her, spooning the length of her body. And unmistakable against her behind was his massive erection. She caught her breath.

Wendy pushed her bottom toward him and loosened her legs, lowering her head onto the headrest of the lounge. She felt him respond by guiding his member between her legs gently and up, the glans of his penis touching the opening of her passage. When he eased it forward, he found it wet—not with water from the spa and pool, but with the nectar of her anticipation. He thrust gradually once, twice, three times, and his cock was fully within her. She sighed and closed her eyes.

Garrett began to move his hips forward and back, gliding deep within. He slid his hand over her arm and caressed her breast, depressing the stalky nipple softly. He seemed to seemed to grow firmer within her and her effluence created a maddeningly arousing sloshing sound.

"Garrett," she whispered.

". . . Yes."

"Make love to me slowly. . . . I want this moment to last . . . because I know . . . I'm going to remember it . . . forever."

His pace slowed slightly. He put his hands on her shoulders and pulsed forward within her deliberately, fully.

She opened her eyes. A small boat was zipping through the harbor, passing the larger ships almost playfully. The shadows of birds descending before the window, sailing straight down and out of view and then reappearing as they coursed rapidly toward the water. The headlights on the streets between her and the ocean stopped and started and raced. And all the while she felt Garrett within her, making love to her as she received his powerful intent.

The climax came upon her suddenly. There was something about the thick phallus stroking her clitoris and the protrusion above it repeatedly and, as if holding on for as long as she could, she could no longer resist the force of his erection and she came. Air burst from her vagina and it tightened around him spontaneously.

"Oh, Garrett! . . . Oh."

And now he was holding his breath and the pace of his thrusts quickened and his cock seemed even harder. He cried out softly and pressed himself against the cheeks of her behind, holding himself as deeply within her as he could.

"God . . . Wendy." He gasped. "Oh god. . . . Oh god."

As they lay together, his arm holding her back against his chest and his penis still within her, it became clear to them that neither wanted to change position. Gradually his ragged breathing diminished and they were as quiet as they were still.

At length she said softly, "Thank you for a wonderful day, Mr. Bolden."

"No," he replied, "thank you, Ms. Marbury. This has been the most beautiful day I can remember. . . . There's only one way I can think of to improve it."

"Do tell? And how's that?"

He drew a breath. "I think we should put our clothes on, go find a really good bottle of wine, go to our room and screw our brains out."

Leaning against him that Sunday afternoon, her eyes closed and remembering how she had giggled at his suggestion, Wendy could not resist the great smile that spread across her face.

As he had promised, Garrett delivered Wendy to her

driveway at 4:30 on Sunday afternoon, half an hour before their father was supposed to bring her daughters home. And totally to her surprise, when they pulled up to her house Wendy saw Aaron's silver SUV sitting on the right side of the driveway where he used to park before he moved out. As Garrett parked his pickup behind Wendy's minivan, she saw the faces of her girls: Tina in the passenger's seat wearing an expression of great dismay and Tasha in the back seat looking confused, frustrated and curious. Aaron himself sat crossways in the driver's seat, his face ripe with judgment and anger.

Fearing a scene as she did, Wendy tried to remain as emotionless as possible as she looked at Garrett. "Thanks for dropping me off. Really, it was a lovely weekend. It was unlike anything I ever experienced."

He gazed at her as she spoke, his eyes narrowing with doubt. "Wendy, do you really want me to leave just now."

She steeled herself, holding back tears. "No. Not really."

He nodded. "Well, how about if I stick around for a few minutes, until Aaron drops off the girls and leaves?"

"That would be so kind of you."

Garrett climbed out of his side of the pickup holding Wendy's overnight bag. A little stab of panic ran through her at the thought that her daughters would know she had been away and spent the night with this man who was just a stranger to them.

She could see Aaron in the car speaking to the girls. The SUV had been running and quietly the passenger and back seat windows rolled down and the engine cut off. Only Aaron got out of the car.

Turning up the sidewalk toward the front door, Wendy whispered, "Thank you for staying."

"This should be interesting," Garrett muttered. She thought she saw a hint of a smile cross his face.

Wendy unlocked the door wordlessly and she and Garrett trooped in, followed by Aaron. It came back to her then just how tall Aaron was, a good two inches taller than Garrett. And he simmered with intensity.

She struggled to decide where in the house to settle for the coming confrontation. The kitchen. All three could sit around the table. She went in and pulled back a chair and sat down. Garrett sat down next to her, leaning back, one arm casually leaning on the table, unperturbed as he watched Aaron.

Aaron did not sit. He stood before them, his arms crossed. He shifted his weight from side to side, like a prosecutor facing a lying defendant on the witness stand, ready to attack. At length he spoke.

"I don't like this at all. . . . I don't like this for a couple reasons. . . . First, it sets one hell of a bad example for our daughters—you going off and shacking up for a couple days with a guy you barely know."

Wendy's voice trembled. "Well you have me there, Aaron. Most of the women you fucked around with had worked with you for months or years."

"I never said any of those relationships you accused me of ever happened!" His voice rose. "And anyway, I'm not their mother."

"Don't bother being coy, you snarky bastard." She felt her confidence—and anger—growing. "There is no comparing your behavior and my behavior. You were a married man, cheating on your wife—with impunity. And I am an unmarried woman."

"Unmarried barely! You couldn't wait for the divorce to be final before you went sneaking off with your pool boy and some cheap thrills."

"Ha. Just because you didn't know where I was doesn't mean I was sneaking—"

Garrett interrupted her, his voice calm. "It means it was none of your fucking business."

Aaron looked down his nose at Garrett, as if he had been addressed by an insolent teenager. "I'll get to you. Right now this is between me and my wife."

"Ex wife," Wendy corrected. "And just let me say, if my daughters are traumatized by any of this it's on you."

"Me?"

"Yes, you, Mr. Toffler. You were the one snooping around in matters that didn't concern you. And you were the one who decided to show up early in hopes my girls would see me arrive with Garrett."

"And they did." He glanced at Garrett. "And while we're talking about swimming pools and their attendants, I have no intention of allowing Mads Madison to service this pool."

A broad smile broke across of Garrett's face.

"That is not your decision to make," Wendy said incredulously. "After all the shit you gave me about how the house—and especially the swimming pool—was my responsibility, what makes you think you have any say in who takes care of it?"

"Because he is an eighteen or nineteen-year-old boy—who spends most of his time being all but naked—and my thirteen-year-old daughter is crazy about him and she is too young to be exposed to that." His face flushed when both Wendy and Garrett began to laugh. "I'm so glad you think this is funny. I'll do whatever I have to to keep him away from her."

"Aaron," Wendy said deliberately, "Mads is gay." When he stared at her uncertainly, she continued. "Gay. G-A-Y. Gay. He likes boys, not girls."

Aaron glanced at the floor, reflecting. "Mads is gay?" He looked up. "Does Tina know?"

Wendy shook her head adamantly. "No she doesn't know. And you're not going to tell her. If you do, I'll scratch out your beady little eyes."

Aaron seemed to gather himself. Defeated by Wendy in his criticisms and fears, he turned his gaze to Garrett. "And then there is you, Mr. Swimming Pool."

Garrett stared at him with no apparent anxiety.

"How quick you were to zoom in and take advantage of a single mother. Just divorced." He looked at Wendy. "You didn't think of it that way did you, that all he really wanted was a good time? That he caught you at a moment when the ink was barely dry on the divorce decree, a time when you were at your most vulnerable?"

Aaron turned in one direction and then the other, waving his arms. "You can accuse me of anything you want, but I never took advantage of a single mom who just lost her marriage."

"Seriously, Aaron." Wendy shook her head.

"You wanted a good time, didn't you buddy? So you just moved right in thinking nothing of it. And you think you got away with it." He seemed enraged. "Well you haven't."

With that he threw a punch, a wild right hand, at Garrett's head. Garrett seemed to have anticipated the blow and, halfway rising to his feet, he caught Aaron's right hand in his left hand. And held it there. Motionless.

The two men stared at one another. Garrett rose fully to his feet. Apparently his grip on Aaron's hand was causing the taller man a fair amount of pain as well as astonishment. Garrett extended his arm and forced Aaron to sit in an empty chair at the table. Then he released Aaron's fist and stood above him.

"Well now let's hear what pool boy has to say, Mr. Toffler." There was no fury or scorn in Garrett's voice, only confidence and calmness. "First of all, I'm going to do you and me a favor by not breaking your jaw—even though I am tired of listening to you and you do have it coming. If I did, your girls would hate me forever and I don't want that.

"So the question is—even though your beautiful ex-wife is perfectly within her rights to spend the weekend with me or anyone she wants to, and even though it was no way any of your business—did I take advantage of a newly divorced woman on the rebound? I don't know the answer to that. You sure don't know the answer to that. Only Wendy knows that . . . and even she may not know it right now."

Garrett sat back down in his chair. "I'm just going to put my cards all on the table here. The way I got it figured, Toffler, when you saw us at the swim meet, you could feel the attraction between Wendy and myself. Even an oblivious asshole like you could sense it. And when you realized that she and I were spending time together—and by the way it was a lovely weekend in every way—you had a certain moment of awakening. You suddenly realized what you had given up. You realized what a dumbass you had been to lose this very fine person. You felt remorse." Garrett shook his hand, as if he was waving away something Aaron was about to say. "You don't have to agree or disagree, still that is really the reason you came over here and waited for her. All of the sudden, you woke up. And now want her back."

He turned his face to Wendy. "The only important question here is, what does Wendy want? Way down deep, I mean. . . . I guess you need to consider whether or not this 'aha moment' your ex-husband has experienced sort of signals the possibility of a new beginning." He shook his head. "You must have seen something in the guy years ago or you would never have married him in the first place. . . . So now you have the chance to start over, to work on your relationship . . . to pick up where you left off with the idea that this time things can be different." He paused and drew a full breath. "Or you can decide that you don't want to go back. That ultimately whatever you had with your ex is gone and you want to go in a different direction."

Garrett turned away, looking around the kitchen as if seeing a new horizon, then looked back at Aaron. "So Wendy has a decision to make. And you and I are going to help her out, pal. Here is what you're going to do and what I'm going to do. We are going to leave her alone. You will not contact her and I will not contact her. We will stay out of her orbit until she decides what it is that's most important to her and she gets ahold of us to let us know what that is. I'm not going to bother Wendy. And you're not going to bother her, or we'll revisit that whole sucker punch you tried to throw."

He swallowed and sighed and stood. "Now I'm going to leave you alone, Ms. Marbury. I hope to hear from you." He took a step toward the kitchen door.

"Wait. Wait a minute." Wendy interrupted him, and when he stopped, she said, "I have a question for you, Garrett." She held his eyes with hers. "I need you to be completely honest with me. Okay?"

". . . I'm always honest with you."

"Okay. . . . This time we spent in Savannah—"

"Savannah!"

"Shut up, Aaron. This time we spent in Savannah, was it like he said? Was it just . . . a good time for you, a chance to have sex with somebody new? Was it a one-shot deal? Or did you intend for us to spend more time together? . . . Are getting up to walk out to leave space for me, like you said, to consider my options? Or are you walking out of my life?"

He studied her face. "Seriously? Are you seriously asking me that, Wendy? . . . Well maybe the best answer I can give is, I love you. Everything about you. . . . And I would describe everything I love about you—and I will if you want—but not in front of this joker. Of course I want to be with you. . . . But it has to be mutual. That is, I it to be good and right for you. And I don't want you to have any regrets."

She gazed at him, then abruptly nodded. "All right then." She turned to Aaron. "I don't need any time off to decide what's best for me or what I want. I want Garrett."

Both the men reacted with surprise.

"Really?" Garrett asked.

"Oh god yes. I've never been treated with such tenderness, affection and genuine intimacy as I have been in the last two days. Never. You think I'm going to trade that for months of counseling and sacrifice in hopes that this guy can sustain what he's feeling now and build on it to make a working relationship? You think I don't know that, once he thinks he's won me back, he won't go out cruising for someone new." She nodded at her lover. "If you're not in a real hurry, Mr. Bolden, I'd love for you to sit down and visit for a few more minutes. And, Aaron. Thanks for bringing the girls home. I think you know the way out."

Chapter Six

The saffron light of two flickering citronella pots did nothing to interfere with the magnificent, massive presence of the Milky Way. It filled the clear night sky above her, seeming almost close enough to touch. Wendy remembered traveling with her parents and sister as a child on vacations to remote places where there was no light pollution to prevent her from being awed by the presence of stars. Indeed it had been all those long years she realized—lying on the thick air mattress, within the double sleeping bag, beside Garrett, aboard his "middle-sized" sailboat—since she had seen the night sky with no artificial light to dilute it.

The boat scarcely rocked, she realized. Lying with her hands behind her head on the inflated pillow, she felt for the periodic lift and settling of the water. It was amazing to her that they could be anchored in an ocean cove 200 yards off the Gulf coastline of Florida and the sailboat could be virtually still on the water.

She had no idea what time it was. What's more, she did not care. The sun would come up in a few hours and Garrett would serve her breakfast as he had served her dinner—already prepared and sealed in plastic containers: fresh fruit and finger food intended to be eaten and enjoyed without being heated. Once again Wendy found herself in the midst of a thoroughly delightful experience Garrett had planned in detail just for the two of them.

She had been on the phone with Laura, her friend who could be called at any hour, when Garrett pulled up in front of her house at 6 that morning.

"Wait a minute, hon. I think somebody just stopped in the street in front of the house." She hurried into the living room and went to the bay window.

"Is it him?" Laura asked. "Tell me he didn't really show up at 6 a.m."

For a moment Wendy said nothing, staring in awe at the boat and trailer hooked to the back of Garrett's truck. "It is him. When he says 6, he means 6."

"And you two are really going sailing? On the ocean? In winter?"

"Yes, yes and yes. Garrett says this will be wonderful. The water and the weather are perfect on the Gulf side."

"The Gulf side?"

"Yes, girlfriend. As opposed to the Atlantic side." She stared at him as he walked around the boat, checking various knots, coupling and enclosures. "He keeps track of all that so he can pick and choose the best locations with the perfect wind and all that. Boy, that boat sure seems awfully big just to be his middle-sized one."

"Well how big is it? His boat I mean."

"I know what you meant, unless you meant something else. It's long. Maybe almost as long as my driveway. I thought it was the trailer that made it look long, but the boat is longer than the trailer."

"What's he wearing?"

Wendy pulled the phone away from herself and looked at it, before holding it against her ear again. "What do you mean 'what's he wearing?' What difference does it make?"

"I'm just, you know, curious. I never went sailing on the ocean in a sailboat."

"Well, he's wearing a long-sleeve t-shirt, blue jeans. And topsiders."

"Are you scared?"

"Oops. He's headed toward the house now. Of course I'm scared. I have to go."

They had headed almost due west of Orlando, traveling Highway 50 toward Hernando Beach. Garrett had coffee and bagels in the cab of the truck. Wendy slathered the bagels with cream cheese and tore them apart, stuffing pieces into his mouth as if he were a baby bird. The hour-and-a-half passed quickly and she was a little stunned to gaze out the windshield and see the Gulf of Mexico before them.

He parked in a boat ramp area and began to rig the boat. She walked around him, totally awed by all he was doing as he raised the mast and fastened various pieces of the rigging together with lanyards, clasps and knots.

"Can I help?" she asked, desperately hoping he would say, "No."

"Just watch. I want you to memorize everything," he replied. "So when we get back you can take it down."

"Oh. . . . Okay. . . . No problem. Where's the . . . you know, the prop thing?"

"You mean the propeller?"

"Yeah, that."

"Oh, dang. I knew I forgot something." He smiled at her. "Actually, since this boat has no motor, a propeller would not do it much good."

"No motor? You mean we're about to go out on the ocean in a boat with no engine?"

"Yep," he said matter-of-factly. "We're the first. Except for Christopher Columbus. John Paul Jones. The Spanish, Portuguese, Dutch and Norwegian explorers. Except for them, we're the first."

"It's just that . . . well, what if we get in trouble out on the ocean?"

"I thought you liked to swim."

"Well, yeah, but not with, you know, sharks and jelly fish. Not all the way across the ocean."

He shook his head, clearly unworried and totally casual. "Here's what you do, love. If the boat capsizes and you come up and I don't, don't start swimming until you turn all the around in a complete circle."

"So I can see the closest land?"

88

"No, so you can see what happened to me and save my ass."

She squinted. "You're teasing me. Just making fun of me. And I'm being completely serious."

"Yeah. But you're so cute when you're scared." He released one final strap securing the boat to the trailer. "Now I'm going to back the boat into the water. You hold onto this bow line. When she starts to float, I'll pull the truck forward and park it. Then we'll be on our way."

They had not sailed a quarter mile away from land before Wendy realized Garrett knew exactly what he was doing and she could not have been in safer hands. After fifteen minutes on the water, they were going faster than she imagined any sailboat could travel. They reclined beside each other in the little scoop behind the tiny cabin and he explained to her how the wind was actually sucking against the sails to make the boat move forward. He used nautical terms and translated them into plain language so she could familiarize herself with the parts of the boat, the description of the wind and the boat's relationship to it.

At one point, an hour or so after they had departed from the dock, he said quietly, "I love to sail. It's as close to flying as you can get without going into the sky. The same rules of aeronautics apply."

She gazed at him. "You're really a romantic at heart. You know this, right?"

He shrugged. "All I know is, it's a real privilege to be able just to be myself with someone. It's a real privilege to be with you."

". . . You really mean that, don't you?" It was less a question than an observation spoken in awe.

"Well of course I mean it."

Because she didn't know what to say, she responded by looping her arms around his arm—something that only lasted for about fifteen seconds before he need both hands to steer the boat closer into the wind.

"Want to go fast?"

"Fast?" she asked. "We've been going amazingly fast."

"Well, we've been on a broad reach," he said. "Now we're going to go closer to the source of the wind, due west-northwest. It's called a narrow reach and it means we're going to have to lard out."

"Do what?"

He pointed to a rail running along the inside of the scoop. "See this? It's not for holding onto. It's for hooking your toes and feet through it from the bottom. Then you hold onto the sheet—"

"Sheet? What sheet?"

"Sheet is what you call rope on a sailboat."

"Oh. What do you call the sail?"

"Sail."

"Oh. This is a lot to learn."

"Well it's about to get real fun. Hook your toes under there and grab hold of something. We're about to lard out."

"What does that mean?"

"It means hang your ass off the edge of the boat. The boat will ride up on its opposite side and we have to lean out backwards over the water to make sure it doesn't roll over."

"Well—well, what if we don't have enough lard?"

"I told you you should have had another bagel. No, seriously, if we start to roll over, either I'll steer us directly into the wind or I'll release the sheet and the tiller and the boat will right itself." Gradually beginning to smile, he watched her. "You ready?"

"Not really."

He laughed. "Prepare to come about, mate."

He turned the wheel and the prow of the boat swung so that the wind was instantly coming from the other side. The boom crossed above her head, but Garrett held the rope tightly as it did. She could feel the boat rise up beneath her and for an instant she thought it would continue rolling and throw them into the ocean.

"Lard out!" Garrett called.

He leaned backward over side of the boat until he was horizontal to the water. Fearfully gripping his arm, she leaned backward as well, closing her eyes. She could feel the boat stabilize itself, riding on its side almost directly into the wind. As they continued, she persuaded herself to open her eyes against the sun and the cool spray.

"Oh my god!" she exclaimed. "We can't be going this fast."

He laughed, a deep, rich, joyful, childlike laugh. "It's kind of fun, isn't it?"

"Oh my god!"

They continued, the boat coursing along with them leaning out over the water, for several minutes. Then Garrett eased the prow slightly away from the direction of the wind and the boat settled evenly onto the water.

"Whew!" she exclaimed. "That was amazing."

"It is awesome. You can't keep it up forever, though."

"'Cause you'll damage the boat?"

"No, love. When you wake up tomorrow morning and try sitting up, you'll understand."

"Oh. . . . Oh no."

He laughed.

It dawned on her that she could not see land in any direction. "Where are we?"

"Well, this is the ocean."

She punched him on his shoulder. "I know that, you thug. Where are we?"

"We are about ten miles west and five miles north of Hernando Beach, lightly making way toward the Florida Panhandle. I'm intending for us to put back east toward the west coast in about an hour for lunch. Unless you have other plans."

Now she laughed. "Actually that's exactly what I was thinking we should do."

By mid afternoon she had become accustomed to the way Garrett maneuvered the boat toward and through the wind. She understood perfectly why he had named the boat *Ballerina*. It responded swiftly to his masterful touch. Then it occurred to her that her body did the same and suddenly, astonishingly, she found herself aroused.

"I'm going to set out away from the coast for the next hour or so," he said. "Pretty soon the sun will begin to set and sailing into it, even with sunglasses is way too hard on your eyes."

The boat made a sharp left turn—or as he had taught her, "hard to port," the boom swinging over her head again. For a long time they sailed in one direction, lying together in the scoop, his arm around her shoulders. It was incredibly serene.

As the sun continued to drop and grow to the point of being oppressively bright, Garrett called, "Prepare to come about, mate."

Again he swung the wheel and the boom crossed above them. This time the boat continued to turn until the sun was almost directly behind them.

"Hold the wheel, will you?" he said without looking at her.

She grabbed it and held it tightly in place as he clambered forward and began working on the rigging. Suddenly a third sail emerged, seeming to burst forth from the mast itself. Shaped like a parachute, it ballooned out before her and settled above the prow so that she could still see the horizon.

"What's that?" she asked as he crawled back to her.

He did not offer to take the wheel. Instead he folded his hands and leaned his back against the scoop beside her.

"Steady as she goes, first officer." He nodded to the new, brilliantly colored sail. "That is the spinnaker. It's used when you have the wind behind you."

"And it's named for your dog?"

"Exactly. Every sloop and racing boat in the world has a sail named for my dog. . . . That's only as it should be. He's a great dog." He stretched. "So I'm going to take a little nap now."

"No you're not!"

"Why not? Maybe I'll go for a swim."

"What's wrong with you?"

"Not a damn thing. You're just so much fun to tease." He pointed to the compass mounted behind the mast. "Just make dead ahead to that setting you're on, east-northeast."

"How long?"

"'Til I wake up."

"No! Don't joke like that."

"Well, if I figured right, about sunset we should be in sight of the mainland. Then we'll find a cove and anchor down for the night." He glanced at her. "How are you doing, mate?"

She smiled. "I don't know why—I mean, I haven't done anything but sit here—but I'm starving. And I'm tired."

"Well you've probably expended more energy than you realize. We'll sleep like babies tonight."

"Sleep where?"

"In the water."

"In the water?"

"Oh, that's right. This is only February, isn't it? Might still be a little chilly. I guess we'll sleep on deck."

". . . Are you still kidding?"

He laughed. "I guess we'll see."

Wendy did hold the wheel steady—mostly—for about an hour, she begged him to take it over eventually so she could look back at the magnificent sunset behind them. It was a surprisingly emotional experience—full of awe and joy, though for some reason she felt like weeping. Garrett turned occasionally to watch her. Though he did not speak, he seemed to understand precisely what she was feeling.

Right on schedule, the western Florida coastline came into

view about dusk. Garrett struck the spinnaker when they were still a mile or more away from land. She watched his sure, expert movements silently. Everything about this man filled her with affection and delight.

When they drew to within a half mile of the coastline, Garrett faced the prow north, running parallel to the land. He studied the variegated foliage until he found an inlet, wide and round, that seemed to suit him. As they approached the tree line, since there was no beach, he deftly struck the remaining two sails and let the boat continue to drift inward.

At a certain point he called to her softly. "Ahoy, first officer. Time to drop anchor."

And with that she heard a gentle splash and almost immediately the boat came to a halt.

Quickly he hung a string of low wattage lights from the rigging and turned them on. Minute by minute the insignificant bulbs replaced the disappearing sunlight. As well, he lit two citronella pots and put them at opposite ends of the boat.

"This time of year the bugs aren't too bad. But this will discourage the hardy ones."

From inside the little cabin he produced the food bins. He plied her with chunks of melon and pineapple, deliciously crispy chips, finger sandwiches with chicken salad and pimento cheese and some kind of delightful pastry she had never tasted before. And as he had all day, he insisted that she drink another pint of cool water.

As she was licking her fingers, he showed her a magnum of wine, the bottle obviously chilled. He held two clear, plastic cups in his other hand.

"It's so hard to know what wine goes with pimento cheese and tortilla chips," he said.

"I'll bet you it tastes wonderful." She gazed at his face as he unwrapped the mouth of the bottle and opened it. "You know, Mr. Garrett Bolden, you're sort of an amazing man."

He poured a cup full of liquid that seemed dark amber in the dull light. "Why do you say that?"

"I was sitting here trying to think if there was any woman—any woman—I knew who wouldn't give her wedding ring and favorite necklace to be sitting here with you, being waited on hand-and-foot, in this incredibly romantic . . . I don't know what to call it. It isn't a 'setting.' It isn't a 'date.' It's . . . is it an adventure?"

"Not to spoil the moment, Ms. Marbury, but damn few of the women I've known are interested in having an adventure like this." He topped his plastic cup with wine and took a sip. "Sitting on a little sailboat some nowhere along the coast of northwest Florida without a real bed, bathroom or entertainment-providing media device within fifty miles; eating with your fingers and drinking wine from a plastic cup. If you like this kind of thing, I think you're pretty much one of a kind." He shook his head. "What a foolish, adventurous woman you are. It will be interesting to see if you are ever willing to do something like this again."

"You underestimate how wonderful this excursion is, Mr. Bolden. . . . I guess I don't know any other man who is capable of sailing this boat and bringing someone here. And you seem to think of every detail. . . . Would I do this again? If you asked me, I would do it again in a heartbeat."

He studied her face. "How strange. And you seem so normal."

She laughed, then shivered. "Wow, when the sun went down, it cooled off."

"Oh yeah. It's amazing isn't it. Out in the sun like we were today, you can forget that technically it's still winter. But when it gets dark, it gets cold. And it's not even 6:30."

"So are we going down and huddle in the little cabin?"

"Oh, not exactly."

He opened the cabin and began to pull storage boxes and equipment onto the deck behind the scoop. Within five minutes he had unfolded a thick air mattress—with built-in pillows—and inflated it with a portable compressor. Then he covered it with a fleece sleeping bag large enough for two people.

"You are amazing, Mr. Bolden. So now we get inside this?"

"Nope. We lie on top." He unfolded a quilt. "Under this. And if we get cold, we get inside. . . . And here—" He held up a flat, silver rectangle, a portable DVD player. "—is our entertainment."

"I thought you said we were 50 miles from the nearest electronic media."

"Well . . . I might have exaggerated to a degree."

Garrett gave her a choice of movies from a sleeve of disks. She was surprised at the selection because it included pictures from several of her favorite stars.

"How did you know I liked these guys?"

"Easy," he said coyly. "When we're making love and you squeal, 'Oh George! Oh Brad! Oh Ryan!' it isn't hard to know who you're pretending I am."

"You liar. I never think about anyone but Garrett Bolden. In fact, I can't imagine anyone being more exciting than you are. You just remember me saying I liked their movies."

They crawled beneath the quilt and watched movies until the battery gave out in the player and there was no more warm, mellow wine in the magnum bottle.

Garrett clicked off the light bulbs and they lay looking upward. As her eyes grew accustomed to the darkness, the stars grew brighter until the sky was ablaze with them.

"Oh my god," she said quietly. "The Milky Way. I haven't seen it since I was a little girl. . . . I had forgotten." She turned to him, his features outlined by the starlight and flickering yellow pots. "You come out here by yourself?"

Staring upward, his voice soft, he said, "Very often. Yes. . . . I watch the weather to wait for the perfect weekend: not too many clouds, a little wind but not too much. . . . Then I sail. . . . And I love it all. I love the cold spray, cutting across the wind, running the boat up on its side, watching the sunset over the ocean. . . . And I love lying here at night . . . looking up at lights that started in this direction before I was born. Some of the starlight we can see tonight started in this direction when our ancestors lived in caves and trees. . . . And when I lie here and look up, I feel like I'm a part of it all. Somewhere, circling around one of those stars is a planet with an ocean and some creature is lying in a boat on that ocean looking up and seeing light that left our sun tens of thousands of years ago . . . and wondering who might be circling our star and looking back." He turned to her. "I'm sorry if I went full geek on you there."

She could not hold back her smile. "I never heard anyone say anything like that before."

"Kind of pathetic, huh?"

"No. Kind of poetic." She gazed up at the heavens. "And when you are out here, you always come alone? You like the solitude."

Garrett shook his head. "I never wanted to be alone. But . . . I always assumed I would be." He seemed to be struggling to find the words to express himself. "For me, Wendy, life is an unknown land just waiting to be explored. I've always wanted to travel, to see places I've never been, to eat food I've never tasted, to hear people speak in tongues I've never heard. . . . Always, always, I thought if I did explore life and this world, I would be doing it by myself. I thought I was too eccentric for anyone to want to be with me on the kind of excursions I dream of taking. And, frankly, I never knew anyone I wanted to take around the world with me."

He turned to her. "And then . . . one morning not so long ago I was testing the water in a residential swimming pool and looked over my shoulder and saw you. . . . You were so spontaneous. So . . . . guileless. So incredibly attractive. So smart. You liked my dog. You even found me attractive. And when I touch you, it's like a fire lights up inside me." He made a popping sound with his lips. "I hope I don't scare you away by telling you I have fantasies of taking you with me to all those mysterious, unknown places."

". . . I will go with you anywhere, Garrett Bolden."

Slowly he began to smile. "I should have known. There should have been no doubt that you were the perfect woman from the moment you spoke your name."

". . . Seriously?"

"Of course. I'm a sailor. And you're Wendy."

She threw her head back, laughing. She found his hand with hers and he guided it to his crotch and the tautness of his erection.

She sighed. "All day long has been a new experience for me. But with this—" She ran her hand inside his pants and gripped his penis, which responded by growing even harder. "—I know exactly what to do."

They rolled toward each other, their mouths meeting first, holding a kiss as they tugged at each other's clothes. She widened her legs as he undid the zipper of her jeans and slid his hands inside her panties, his fingers toying with the damp pubic hair and caressing the slick clitoris. She tightened her thighs on his hand, holding his fingers within the lips of her labia as she slid his pants down over his hips. Garrett ran his free hand up her back, beneath her sweat shirt and blouse, deftly unclasping her bra—just as he had expertly worked the rigging on the *Ballerina* all day. His hand went to her breast, cupping it, caressing it, his fingers gliding around the areola and coaxing the nipple into a stalk.

They broke their kiss and anxiously pulled off their clothes, meeting once again in the middle of the air mattress. Garrett disappeared beneath the quilt. She felt his lips on her nipple, one hand holding her behind in place as the fingers of his other hand entered her, his thumb on the man-in-the-boat, massaging it as his fingers slid in and out.

"Oh my. Oh my," she whispered in surprise, "I'm going to come."

And she did, marvelously, quiveringly, the effluence of her nectar flowing forth between her upper thighs. Then, before she had recovered from the electric thrill of the orgasm, Garrett slid down, forcing her legs apart, his feet and calves sticking out from the end of the quilt and his mouth on her vagina.

"Oh!"

His tongue was hot against her clitoris. It forced its way into her passage, exploring, tasting. She put her hand on his head, for an instant intent on pushing him away—instead pressing his face against her crotch.

"Oh. . . . Garrett."

As his tongue maneuvered her enflamed clit from side to side, his middle finger searched upward for the thick pad above it and began to move forward and back. Irresistibly she raised and lowered her hips to his touch, her eyes closed, her head lying to one side limply. She could feel the orgasm coming a full minute before it racked her vagina and abdomen and chest and limbs. Then she lay still, aware only of the weight of his head on her belly and her shaky breathing.

At length she spoke. "Garrett, this has been such a marvelous day. You have waited on me hand and foot. You've fed me and entertained me, and I certainly have no reason to ask you for anything more. . . . However, if it's not too much trouble, would you be willing to fuck me now, dear?"

He raised his head, looking toward her face. "Oh, the pleasure would be all mine, love."

His course tongue found her tingling nipples as he made his way up her body. She could feel his engorged member dragging along the inside her calf, then thigh, then straightening of its own accord as it drew close to her expectant lips. She parted her legs as she felt him enter her and arched her neck as his face descended to hers and they kiss as he rode fully within her and rocked back and forth with excruciating, exhilarating slowness.

She heard herself speaking. "F-u-c-k."

"Something tells me . . . the pleasure . . . isn't all mine."

Moments later urgency seemed to seize him and his movements increased dramatically and then again. His chest heavy on her chest, their bodies sealed together all down their length, he thrust himself into her again and again. Her passage spasmed then, tightening on his member as if to hold him within her and the grip of it slowed his motion just as he climaxed. Wordlessly he held himself within her. She could feel the throbbing of his penis with his ejaculation, filling her, yearning for her. Wendy pulled him down onto to her and held him within and against her, listening to his ragged breathing.

And hours later, as Garrett slept beside her, her hands behind her head, her eyes upon the stars, the thought of their lovemaking aroused her once again. She could wake him, she knew, and he would make love to her again. She smiled. Better to wait. When the sun came up, if not before, he would awaken with a powerful erection. And they would make love. Real love. Because, as both of them knew, they were in love.

How odd, she thought, to have taken this risk so soon after she was free. She had risked diving into the deep end and found more than she had ever known she was missing.

www.ingramcontent.com/pod-product-compliance
Lightning Source LLC
Chambersburg PA
CBHW070345130626
46556CB00007B/3038

* 9 7 8 1 6 3 0 6 6 4 7 3 2 *